This h

329

DOCTOR WHO AND THE
CLAWS OF AXOS

D1476425

DOCTOR WHO
AND THE
CLAWS OF AXOS

Based on the BBC television serial by
Bob Baker and David Martin by arrangement with
the British Broadcasting Corporation

Terrance Dicks

Number 10 in the Doctor Who Library

CENTRAL REGIONAL SCHOOL LIBRARY SERVICE

TARGET

A TARGET BOOK

published by
the Paperback Division of
W. H. Allen & Co. PLC

A Target Book

Published in 1977
by the Paperback Division of
W. H. Allen & Co. PLC
44 Hill Street, London W1X 8LB

Reprinted 1979
Reprinted 1980
Reprinted 1982
Reprinted 1984
Reprinted 1985

Novelisation copyright © Terrance Dicks 1977
Original script copyright © Bob Baker and Dave Martin 1971
'Doctor Who' series copyright © British Broadcasting Corporation 1971,
1977

Printed and bound in Great Britain by
Cox & Wyman Ltd, Reading

ISBN 0 426 11703 4

This book is sold subject to the condition that it shall
not, by way of trade or otherwise, be lent,
re-sold, hired out or otherwise circulated without the
publisher's prior consent in any form of
binding or cover other than that in which it is published
and without a similar condition including this
condition being imposed on the subsequent purchaser.

Contents

1

Invader from Space

It moved through the silent blackness of deep space like a giant jellyfish through the depths of the sea. Its shape was constantly changing, pulsating with energy and life, and a myriad of colours flickered over its glistening surface. Unerringly it sped towards its chosen target, the planet known as Earth. Soon the instruments of the humans would detect its approach. It knew this, and was undisturbed. Detection was the first stage in its plan ...

The tracking station dozed peacefully in the early morning silence. The huge radar aerials revolved in their constant searching, silhouetted against the blue of the sky. In an instrument-packed room, deep inside the building, the results of that search showed up as a blip of light, tracing its curving course across a radar display screen. A man was studying the blip, muttering to himself as he checked the instruments all round him. 'About one million miles ... mass variable ...' He looked again at the dials, shaking his head. '*Variable?* What's the book say, Harry?'

Beside him, his assistant was immersed in a pile of star charts and periodicity tables. 'Nothing here.'

'You sure? There's got to be!'

Harry was bored, irritable, and in no mood for

mysteries at the end of a long and tiring shift. 'Look, there's nothing here. No comets, nothing!'

Pleased, his superior leaned back in his swivel chair. 'Then it looks as if we've discovered a new one! Run another course check.'

While Harry busied himself with the instruments, the senior technician watched the steady progress of the blip. Ransome's Comet, he was thinking happily. Though probably the Director would pinch all the credit, even if he *was* still home in bed. Suddenly Ransome sat up. The blip on the screen had changed direction. 'You get that?'

Harry nodded. 'Picked it up on the instruments. That thing's just altered course.'

'But it *can't* have ...'

With gloomy satisfaction Harry studied a computer print-out. 'You can say goodbye to your comet, mate. Whatever that thing is, it's now on a collision course for Earth!'

Harry reached for a phone, but Ransome put out a hand to stop him. 'What are you doing?'

'Just in case you've forgotten, there's a whole batch of people we're supposed to tell about "Unidentified Flying Objects".' Harry pointed to a list of names and telephone numbers on a nearby notice board. 'The Director, the Ministry of Security ... and something called UNIT—the United Nations Intelligence Task-force.'

Ransome looked at the radar screen a moment longer, saying goodbye to his dream of scientific immortality. Then he sighed and picked up the telephone. 'Get me the Director, please. Red Alert. Yes I know he's still home in bed. Wake him up. Tell him there's an Unidentified Flying Object heading straight for Earth!'

In the military and scientific complex that formed UNIT Headquarters, Brigadier Lethbridge-Stewart's day was getting off to a very bad start. The cause of his present troubles was not alien monsters but Earth-bound bureaucrats. Whitehall's latest brainchild was the newly-created Ministry of Security, an organisation designed to gather all Britain's various intelligence organisations under one central umbrella. The Brigadier had refused to be gathered, taking the position that UNIT was not a national but an international organisation, and as such answerable only to UNIT H.Q. in Geneva. The war of letters, memos and reports had continued for some time now, with the Brigadier more than holding his own. But now the Whitehall enemy had wearied of the paper bombardment and sent in their shock troops—in the stocky and unattractive shape of Horatio Chinn.

Like many small men in high positions, Chinn liked to think of himself as Napoleonic. He saw himself as a hard-driving human dynamo, cutting through the restraints of red tape. He was a vain and rather stupid man, but he was also ruthlessly ambitious and tirelessly energetic. Chinn eventually overcame most of his opponents by wearing them down.

He had even worn down the Minister in charge of his own Department, who couldn't stand the man but couldn't think how to get rid of him. Wily old politician that he was, the Minister had been struck by a sudden brainwave. He had two main problems at the moment—Chinn and the Brigadier. Why not turn them loose on each other? Whichever proved the winner, the Minister would have one less problem to worry about.

The result of this brilliant strategy had been Chinn's appointment as a one-man Committee of Enquiry. It was now Chinn's second day with UNIT, and while the Minister back in Whitehall basked in unaccustomed peace, the Brigadier was already brooding on emergency court-martials and summary executions. If only there was a war on, he thought wistfully, he could lock the fellow up, or even shoot him. Deciding that Chinn was definitely one of the horrors of peace, the Brigadier looked with disfavour at his unwanted guest. Chinn stood by an open filing cabinet, leafing through the files of UNIT personnel. He looked the picture of the perfect bureaucrat. Expensive pin-stripe suit, pink face, grey hair, heavy black horn-rimmed spectacles. Bowler hat, umbrella and briefcase were at the ready on a nearby chair.

Chinn put Josephine Grant's file back into the cabinet, making a mental note that the girl was clearly too young and too inexperienced for security work. A nice little black mark to go into his report on the Brigadier. He lifted out another file, read the name on the cover and opened it. Then he looked up at the Brigadier, his face outraged. 'Is this some kind of joke?'

The blindfold over his eyes, the last cigarette, thought the Brigadier dreamily. Or maybe a last memo would be better for a civil servant ... Aware that Chinn was speaking, the Brigadier dismissed his imaginary firing-squad. 'I'm sorry, Mr Chinn. You were saying?'

'I asked if this was some kind of joke. On the front of this file there are just two words "The Doctor". And inside ...' Chinn flapped the file angrily. 'Nothing!'

A little guiltily, the Brigadier recollected that he'd intended to create a full set of documents for the Doctor when he'd joined UNIT at the time of the first Auton Invasion. Hence the file. But with one crisis following another the matter had been overlooked. Although the Doctor was now known to a select circle as UNIT's Scientific Adviser, he still had no official existence—at least, not on paper.

The Brigadier smiled blandly, playing for time. 'Very astute of you to notice, Mr Chinn. The Doctor's file, is, as you say, empty—for security reasons.'

Chinn felt a glow of satisfaction. At last he had found an issue on which he could join battle. Moreover, it was a case where the Brigadier was clearly in the wrong. 'May I remind you, Brigadier,' he began pompously, 'that I am conducting an official enquiry on behalf of the Minister for Security?'

'And may I remind you, Mr Chinn, that UNIT does not come under the Minister's authority?'

Stalemate. Chinn tried again. 'Surely as a matter of elementary organisation, *all* security personnel must be properly screened ...'

The Brigadier smiled. 'And scrupulously filed. Quite so. But the Doctor is a special case.'

'I insist on seeing a proper file for this Doctor— whoever he is!'

'I'm sorry, Mr Chinn. The Doctor is my personal responsibility.'

Chinn slammed the filing cabinet drawer with a bang. 'You seem to think UNIT is your own private army, Brigadier. Not so! Emphatically not so. You are funded, in part, by the British Government. As their representative, I demand your full co-operation.'

Chinn had found these sudden calculated outbursts of rage an effective means of getting his own way. Unfortunately the Brigadier seemed quite unintimidated. Positively uninterested, in fact. Chinn changed his approach. 'Surely, Brigadier, you can see that better liaison with the Government is in your interests, as well as ours? Now, who is this Doctor? Where does he come from? Is he a British subject?'

Thoughtfully the Brigadier stroked his clipped moustache. How did you explain to someone as mentally limited as Chinn that the subject of his enquiry was not only not British, he wasn't even human? That he had formerly been in the habit of travelling through Space and Time in an old blue police box called the TARDIS? That after a complete transformation in his appearance, he was now exiled to Earth by his mysterious superiors, the Time Lords?

The answer was, thought the Brigadier, you did no such thing. Not unless you wanted to be carted off in a strait-jacket.

The door was flung open and a tall white-haired man strode into the room. He was wearing what appeared to be some form of fancy dress. Chinn got a confused impression of velvet jacket, ruffled shirt, even some kind of cloak ... The deeply lined face was curiously youthful, the bright blue eyes blazed with energy and intelligence. The newcomer slipped the cloak from his shoulders and tossed it carelessly onto a chair. 'Morning, Brigadier,' he said cheerily. Leaning casually against the filing cabinet, he looked benignly down at Chinn. 'And who might you be?'

The Brigadier rose from behind his desk. 'This is Mr Chinn from the Ministry,' he said smoothly. 'Mr Chinn—allow me to introduce the Doctor!'

Hurriedly assembling papers in her cubby-hole of an office, Jo Grant realised that, not for the first time, she was going to be late for the Brigadier's morning conference. She threw open the door, rushed out and bounced straight off a man who was trying to come in. Jo and the papers went flying in different directions. Calmly the stranger picked up first Jo and then the papers. He handed them back and waited patiently while Jo dusted herself down. He was somewhere in his early thirties, not tall but with an air of compact strength about him. He had closely trimmed brown hair and a pleasantly ugly face. He wore a dark-grey lightweight suit, and clutched a slim square briefcase. When he spoke his voice had a soft American drawl. 'You all right now, young lady? I'm looking for a fellow called Joe Grant.'

'I'm fine, thanks. What can I do for you?'

The American smiled down at her. She was a pretty little kid, fair-haired, blue-eyed, trendily dressed. She looked far too young to be working in Intelligence. Clearly she hadn't understood his question. 'I'm looking for Joe Grant,' he repeated.

Jo smiled. 'You're looking *at* her,' she corrected. 'Jo, short for Josephine.'

The American made a rapid mental readjustment.

If the British wanted to employ kids in their Intelligence set-up it was no affair of his. 'Well, O.K. In that case, we're both looking for the Brigadier, right?'

'Right! And you're the new liaison officer from Washington. They told me you were coming.'

The American held out his hand. 'I'm Bill Filer. Pleased to meet you.'

Jo returned the handshake. 'Follow me. I'll take you to our leader!'

As they walked along the corridor she said, 'I gather Washington was worried about our not catching the Master?'

Filer said tactfully, 'Well, something like that.'

'And you're going to deal with him single-handed?'

'You're thinking of Errol Flynn!'

'Who?'

Filer grinned. 'I must be getting old!'

As they approached the door to the Brigadier's office they heard the sound of raised voices ...

Chinn's attempts to cross-question the Doctor had met with little success. Disliking both his tone and manner the Doctor had recommended Chinn to mind his own business, and thereafter ignored him, burying himself in a pile of scientific papers. Now thoroughly enraged, Chinn was haranguing the Brigadier. 'Since no records exist for this man, he has no official existence. I demand that you suspend him from his duties.'

The Doctor looked up. 'Oh yes? How can you suspend someone who doesn't exist in the first place?'

Unable to think of a logical answer, Chinn ignored him. 'Brigadier, you must see the scandal this could cause? This is a top-security organisation, yet one of your own advisers is nothing less than ...' He spluttered into silence, having no real idea of *what* the Doctor might really be ...

The Doctor finished his sentence for him. 'An alien? Oh yes, I'm an alien, more alien than you could possibly imagine.' Suddenly the Doctor became very angry. Throwing down his papers he jumped to his feet, towering menacingly over Chinn. 'Suspend me if you like, Mr Chinn. Do you think I'd mind leaving this organisation? I'd happily leave the entire planet—if only to get away from people like you with your petty localised obsessions ...'

Terrified, Chinn struggled to regain his self-possession. 'I have a duty to my country ...'

'To your country?' thundered the Doctor. 'What about your duty to the world? To the galaxy, if it comes to that ...'

As the Doctor and Chinn went on shouting at each other, the door opened and Jo Grant popped her head inside the room.

'Sorry to interrupt, but Mr Filer's arrived from Washington. Has the conference started yet?'

The Brigadier bellowed, 'Does it sound like it, Miss Grant? Bring Mr Filer in by all means, the more the merrier.'

Rather nervously, Bill Filer edged into the room, wondering how he'd ever got the impression that the British were calm and reserved.

His arrival cooled everyone down, and hurried introductions were performed. In the awkward silence that followed Jo said, 'I thought we were here to discuss the Master?'

Chinn was immediately alert. 'Master? Who's the Master?'

The Brigadier sighed. Explaining the Master was almost as difficult as explaining the Doctor. A renegade member of the Doctor's own Time Lord race, the Master had followed the Doctor to Earth on a mission of vengeance, helping the invading Nestenes on their second attempt to conquer Earth. After the invasion had been defeated the Master had vanished. Some time later he had reappeared in the guise of a prominent criminologist, making a second attempt to destroy the Doctor and conquer the Earth. When this too was defeated, the Master had vanished yet again. But by now his name, if little else about him, was on the files of several world intelligence agencies. The Americans, alarmed by vague rumours of some supercriminal on the loose, had sent Bill Filer on a factfinding mission. The Brigadier hadn't really been looking forward to Filer's arrival. There was little enough to tell about the Master, and what there was the Americans probably wouldn't believe.

Filer was unlocking his briefcase. 'I have a file of several top criminals and enemy intelligence operatives in America,' he announced solemnly. 'Our people thought maybe one of them could be this Master guy.'

The Doctor, his anger apparently forgotten, was gazing abstractedly out of the window at the woods and lawns that surrounded UNIT H.Q. He spoke without turning round. 'There's absolutely no point in discussing the Master. He's probably left Earth by now.'

Filer gave the Doctor's back a baffled look, then

turned to the Brigadier. 'If we could just check, sir?'

The Brigadier nodded. 'By all means, Mr Filer.' He glanced at the silent figure by the window. 'After all, Doctor, we can't be certain he's, er, moved on. We've got to go on looking.'

Chinn was jumping up and down with impatience. Everyone seemed to be ignoring him. 'Will someone kindly tell me—who is the Master?'

Filer hesitated. 'I'm afraid that's classified,' he said politely. 'If you don't know already, then you obviously don't have clearance.'

'I assure you, young man, I have been guaranteed full access.'

'Not by us, sir,' interrupted Filer firmly. 'I'm afraid you're a security risk!'

The Doctor swung round, smiling. 'Well, well, well! How does it feel, Mr Chinn?'

Perhaps fortunately, there was yet another interruption before Chinn could reply. The door burst open and a fair-haired young army officer rushed into the room. He skidded to a halt, and gave the Brigadier a hurried salute. 'Sorry to interrupt, sir.'

'All right, Captain Yates, what is it?'

Mike Yates was breathless with excitement. 'Unidentified Flying Object, sir. Fully confirmed sighting, coming in fast. They think it's going to attack!'

2

The Landing

'UFO bearing two zero nine ... five hundred miles and closing ... velocity twenty m.p.s., decreasing ... mass variable ...'

'Sightings confirmed ... Houston, held and tracking ... Hawaii held and tracking ...' There was an atmosphere of tense excitement in the UNIT operations room, and the babble of the technicians' voices filled the air. The long room was filled with ultra-modern communications equipment. In one corner a computer terminal chattered busily as it reeled out yards of print-out. Centre of everyone's attention was the big radar screen which showed the mysterious blip moving steadily closer to Earth ...

Captain Yates turned to the burly figure of Sergeant Benton, who was supervising the scene. 'What's the picture now, sergeant?'

'Negative on asteroid, sir. They're running a missile check.'

Chinn pushed his way to the front of the group. 'Missile? What's all this about a missile?'

The Brigadier gave him an impatient glance. 'An Unidentified Flying Object appears to be heading for Earth. Shouldn't you be in touch with your Ministry, Mr Chinn?'

Chinn nodded emphatically. 'A telephone at once, if you please, Brigadier.'

Captain Yates was about to hand Chinn the nearest free telephone receiver when the Brigadier shook his head meaningfully.

'Show Mr Chinn the *direct* line, Captain Yates—the one over there!'

Suppressing a smile, Captain Yates said, 'This way please, Mr Chinn.' He led Chinn to a cubicle in the far corner of the room. The cubicle actually held a perfectly ordinary telephone—but it was far enough away to keep Chinn out of the Brigadier's hair.

The Brigadier looked at the blip on the screen. 'Well, Doctor—what is it?'

The Doctor shook his head, 'I haven't the slightest idea, old chap.'

A radar technician snapped. 'Course changing now, sir. Bearing two zero seven.'

The Doctor was studying a computer print-out. 'Variable mass, eh? Most interesting!'

The technician's voice became more urgent. 'Orbital flight path ... UFO entering Earth's atmosphere ... now!' There was a brief flare-up on the radar screen, then the blip continued its steady course.

Jo tugged the Doctor's sleeve. 'Is it going to land?'

The Doctor moved across to a large wall-map of the British Isles. 'Oh yes. Somewhere on the south-east coast I should imagine.'

The technician said, 'UFO over South Atlantic, sir.'

Chinn pushed his way to the front of the screen, glowing with self-satisfaction. 'The Minister has appointed me co-ordinator of this operation. He wants your communications facilities linked to strike command immediately. I have full authority.' Chinn was under no illusions as to the reasons for his sudden promotion. The Minister had decided that this was an extremely tricky situation, and had shuffled off responsibility as soon as possible. But Chinn didn't mind responsibility. He had the power now—and he was going to use it.

The Brigadier looked thoughtfully at Chinn, realising he had underestimated the man. Now Chinn had gone over his head—and the crisis was too close to wrangle about chains of command. He nodded to Captain Yates who said quietly, 'All taken care of, sir. We're already linked-up to the missile base.'

The Doctor rejoined the group. 'May we ask what you intend to do—Co-ordinator?'

'I have been informed that several attempts have been made to communicate with this object. It does not respond. My orders are that unless it alters course, it is to be totally destroyed.'

'The usual policy, I suppose,' snapped the Doctor. 'Shoot first, ask questions later!'

For once the Brigadier was on Chinn's side. 'There's not much alternative, Doctor. In the absence of other evidence, we must presume that the object is hostile.'

Chinn was talking into the red telephone. 'Station Commander? I want you ready to destroy this thing the moment I give the word. Stand by.'

The technician's voice came again. 'Target area confirmed. England. South-east coast.' Everyone glanced at the Doctor, who looked aggravatingly smug. but said nothing.

The technician's voice broke the tense silence.

'UFO course steady, velocity decreasing, decreasing, decreasing ...' The blip on the screen slowed until it seemed almost motionless.

Chinn shouted down the phone. 'Missile strike *now*, Commander. Now!'

Seconds later a cluster of tiny dots appeared on the bottom of the radar screen, moving steadily towards the larger blip in the centre. Chinn rubbed his hands. 'Perfect! A sitting target!'

The Doctor rubbed his chin. 'Hardly seems sporting, does it?'

Chinn was just about to make an angry retort— when the blip in the centre of the screen suddenly disappeared.

'Contact lost. Contact lost!' There was unbelieving panic in the technician's voice. 'The thing's— gone!'

'Destroyed!' said Chinn in satisfied tones.

Frantically the technician shook his head. 'You don't understand, sir. The missiles haven't even reached it yet. Look!' On the screen the cluster of missiles streaked steadily on into empty space.

The Doctor tapped Chinn on the shoulder. 'Don't you think you'd better abort? What goes up must come down, you know!'

Chinn stared dazedly at him.

The Doctor said sharply, 'The missiles, man. For heaven's sake, abort!'

Chinn stumbled to the phone. 'Station commander. Abort mission. I said *abort*!'

The cluster of dots vanished from the screen, as the missiles exploded harmlessly in space.

The Brigadier looked almost indignantly at the

Doctor. 'It can't just have vanished, Doctor. Where's it gone?'

The Doctor was back at the wall map. 'It hasn't *gone* anywhere—it's *arrived*. If my calculations are correct, we shall find it just about ... here!'

The Doctor's long finger touched a precise spot on the map. The Brigadier stared incredulously at him. Then he roared. 'Captain Yates! Sergeant Benton! Red Alert! I want a full task force on the move right away!'

Yates and Benton sprinted from the room.

Old Josh rode his ancient rusty bicycle down the rutted lane, muttering and grumbling to himself as he pedalled along. Old Josh always had something to grumble about. There had been a lot of changes in recent years, and he didn't much care for any of them. The biggest and worst change of all had been the building of some enormous new-fangled scientific complex, slap in the middle of the marshes, and right between Josh's tumbledown cottage and the nearest pub. Since the complex was completely fenced off, Josh had to ride an extra two miles to get to his beer. He cursed the scientists and their buildings every thirsty inch of the way.

Josh was rounding the curve by Ducket's Pond when it happened. A sudden bright light, an ear-shattering whistle, a massive shape cutting off the sun. Josh gave a shout of rage and fear, and rode his bike straight into the pond.

Luckily for Josh, the water, although murky, was fairly shallow. He surfaced in a shower of mud and duckweed. Disentangling himself from his bike, he staggered out of the pond, dragging the old machine after him. Once on the bank he shook himself like a dog after a swim and looked round for the cause of his accident. He felt pretty sure it was all the fault of 'them scientists', and enticing thoughts of financial compensation began to form in his mind. Blowing a man clear off his bike! That ought to be worth a few quid.

Shading his eyes with his hand, Old Josh peered round. Just behind a clump of trees, a column of dust and smoke was drifting skywards. Guessing that this was the scene of the mysterious accident, Josh started wheeling his bike across country. As he came round the edge of the trees he stopped in astonishment. Just before him, in the centre of a patch of open marshland, was an irregular humped shape, as if a low hill had appeared from nowhere. At first Josh thought some giant meteorite had fallen from the skies and buried itself in the ground. But as he came closer to the mound, he saw that it wasn't made of stone. It was hard to see what it *was* made of—the lumpy mottled surface seemed to reflect the light in several colours at once, and the thing looked *grown* rather than made. Josh touched it cautiously then snatched back his hand. Dratted thing was *hot*!

Cautiously Josh began walking round his discovery. It took him several minutes to make the full circuit, and he ended up where he'd started, none the wiser. There were no openings, no markings, just the same mottled, lumpy surface all the way round.

Water forming a puddle around his feet, Josh gazed

thoughtfully at the mysterious object. Whatever it was, it was news. Josh had visions of free-spending journalists crowding into his favourite pub, buying pints all round—not to mention a handful of fivers for the lucky eyewitness ...

Josh was so intent on turning his experience to profit it didn't occur to him the object might have plans of its own. He didn't notice the thick, vine-like tentacle as it emerged from the base of the mound and crawled slowly towards him. Suddenly, the tentacle reared up, wrapped itself round his body and dragged him towards the mound ... He struggled uselessly for a moment, then went limp, fainting from sheer terror. An opening appeared in the mound, like a gaping mouth, and Josh disappeared inside. The gap closed behind him, and all was quiet.

When he came to, minutes later, he was in the heart of a nightmare. A network of tentacles held him flat on his back, powerless to move. A giant eye on a flexible stalk peered down at him. Multi-coloured lights played over his face, and an eerie throbbing filled the air. A cold, clear, sibilant voice filled the space all around him. 'Analysis pattern reveals ... locomotor facility normal ... sensory receptors acute ... intelligence quotient atypically low.' There was a moment's pause, then the Voice of Axos delivered its final judgement. 'This specimen is valueless. Absorb, process and eject.'

The tentacles tightened their grip and Josh went rigid as all life and energy were instantly drawn out of him. He opened his mouth to scream but no sound emerged. His face dried and *cracked* like a river bed in times of drought. A gap opened beneath him and Axos absorbed him once more ...

Chinn jabbed a finger at the map. By now he had recovered from his shock, and his Napoleonic streak was emerging once more. 'We can be certain that this thing is hostile. According to your own calculations, Doctor, it's landed right beside the national power complex. Britain's entire power supply is menaced. Such a choice of landing site *cannot* be accidental.'

The Brigadier felt forced to admit that Chinn seemed to have a point. The Nuton Power Complex was the vital first step in Britain's use of atomic power for domestic and industrial supply. From one enormous nuclear reactor, power was chanelled to outlets all over the country. The fact that of all possible sites, the thing had plonked itself down beside the Nuton Reactor seemed suspicious in the extreme.

Sergeant Benton clattered back into the room looking tough and efficient in his combat uniform. 'Task Force ready to move, sir. The men are waiting in the assembly area.'

'We'll be right with you. Doctor, shall we go?'

The Doctor nodded and followed the Brigadier to the door. Jo and Filer started to go with them, but Chinn suddenly raised his hand.

'One moment, Mr Filer. This is a purely internal matter, and your presence is unnecessary. I suggest you report back to your own people.'

Filer stood quite still. Encouraged by his quietness, Chinn went on, 'I must warn you that unless you leave immediately. I shall have you placed under arrest.'

The Brigadier was outraged at this treatment of an ally. 'Now look here, Chinn,' he began.

Filer interrupted. 'It's O.K., Brigadier,' he said soothingly. 'I wouldn't want to cause any friction.' He took a long hard look at the wall-map, then moved towards the door. 'Goodbye, Mr Chinn. Take care!' He slipped quietly from the room.

Once he was out of the door, Bill Filer made for the car-park at a run. He knew exactly what the Brigadier's next move would be—he'd clear the entire area around the UFO landing site and seal it off with a cordon of troops. Once that cordon was in place it would be a major operation to get past it, especially with that guy Chinn gumming up the works. But if a man could get to the site *before* the cordon, he'd be right on the spot from the beginning. Filer reckoned that a UFO landing in England was something that concerned America too. When he reported back to Washington it was going to be with every possible scrap of information.

As he jumped into his car Filer knew he had only a few minutes lead. Already the UNIT lorries were almost ready to move off, engines running as the last few armed men leaped on board. Filer swung his dark-green Ford ahead of the convoy, out of the car-park and roared down the road towards the coast.

He pushed the powerful car to its limits, thankful it was winter rather than summer and traffic on the coastal road was light. He'd expected to find curious crowds in the Nuton area, but as he drove through the marshlands everything seemed quiet and deserted. Soon the Nuton buildings came in sight, gleaming like some science fiction city across the marshes, encircled by their high perimeter fence. Filer summoned up a mental picture of the UNIT map. If the Doctor's calculations were correct, the UFO had landed somewhere to the north-west of the main complex.

Reducing speed to a crawl, Filer drove slowly around the complex, eyes searching the flat, desolate country about him. There was nothing to see, just deserted marshland with a few clumps of trees. Then suddenly he saw it, an irregularly shaped mound close by a clump of trees. It didn't look much like a spaceship—but if the UFO had buried itself in the soft ground ...

Filer swung his car off the road, jolted it across the marshes and parked in the middle of the clump of trees. Jumping out, he began walking cautiously towards the mound.

Just beside it, he stumbled over a rusty old bike lying on its side. Filer scratched his head. *Maybe* the thing had been here all along ... Or maybe he wasn't the first to examine the strange mound. And in that case, what had happened to the guy with the bike?

Like Old Josh before him, Filer made a cautious examination of the mound. He touched the strange mottled surface, cooling rapidly now, but still warm to the touch. Filer thought he could detect a faint throbbing, as if the thing were alive.

Again like Josh, Filer walked around the mound, returning eventually to his starting point. He stood looking at the mound, scratching his head. He had a swift mental picture of the way they'd react in Washington if he came back with a report that the British had been invaded by a giant pumpkin from outer space. The roar of vehicles interrupted his thoughts—UNIT was right on his tail. Instinctively he flung himself to the ground and wriggled into cover of the trees.

Prone behind a tree-trunk, Filer watched the arrival of the UNIT convoy. No sooner had the lorries stopped moving than armed troops jumped down and began spreading out in a cordon, encircling the entire area. Filer saw Yates and Sergeant Benton directing the men into their positions.

Two more vehicles drove up and parked near the convoy. The first was ultra-modern, a huge gleaming vehicle about the size and shape of an outsize furniture van, with a forest of aerials projecting from its roof. Some kind of Mobile H.Q., guessed Filer. Probably a portable laboratory packed with electronic scanning devices. By contrast, the second vehicle was small and very old fashioned. It was a vintage Edwardian roadster, and from it descended the Doctor and Jo Grant. They surveyed the busy scene around them for a moment, then made for the mobile H.Q.

Last vehicle to arrive was a huge, gleaming staff car. The doors opened and Chinn, the Brigadier, a man in a dark suit and another in sports jacket and flannels jumped out, all arguing furiously. Chinn ushered them towards the Mobile H.Q. and they too disappeared inside.

Filer lay flattened in his hiding place, wondering what to do next. There seemed little chance of learning very much more where he was now. And he'd feel distinctly foolish if one of the UNIT soldiers found him hiding behind a tree. But if he went to the Mobile H.Q. Chinn would have him arrested ...

Before Filer could make up his mind, the decision was taken for him. The tentacle had been creeping nearer for some time. In a final lunge it wrapped itself round Filer's body and dragged him towards the mound ...

Seconds later, Filer, like Josh before him, lay pinioned and helpless in the heart of Axos. The single eye on its long stalk hovered horribly above him, and multi-coloured lights played over his face. But this time the cold whispering voice reached a different conclusion. 'Subject intelligent, aggressive, possibly dangerous. Hold for further analysis and investigation.'

There was a crackle of energy and Filer felt consciousness slipping away ...

3

The Voice of Axos

Inside the Mobile H.Q., technicians were busily scanning the mysterious mound nearby. The Doctor, clipboard in hand, was studying instrument-readings, jotting down notes with a frown of concentration on his face. He didn't look up when the Brigadier and his party bustled in. Formal as ever, the Brigadier made introductions. 'Doctor, this is Sir George Hardiman, Administrative Head of the Nuton Power Complex. This is Doctor Winser, Head of Research.' The Doctor gave a brief nod, and went on working. The Brigadier coughed. 'The Doctor is our Scientific Adviser.' Hardiman and Winser looked politely baffled. They were two very different types, thought Jo. The first, immaculate in his dark suit, was very much the administrator, a man at home in board rooms and Government offices. Winser was more casually dressed. Tall and thin, he looked surprisingly young for his eminent position. He had a keen, beaky-nosed face, and untidy fair hair.

As if continuing a previous argument, Winser spoke urgently to the Brigadier. 'You must see that any form of military attack so close to the labs could be extremely dangerous.'

Hardiman joined in to support his colleague. 'And as well as the research laboratories, most of Britain's nuclear energy resources are concentrated less than half a mile from this spot!'

The Brigadier snapped, 'At the moment we've no idea what we're up against. We are merely taking necessary precautions. I've been in touch with the Regular Army—they'll be bringing up some artillery support.'

'Artillery!' The Doctor's voice was scornful. 'Your missiles weren't much use, were they? What chance have your bazookas?' Suddenly he changed the subject. 'Winser, did you say? I read a copy of your paper, "Relativity Phenomena in Particle Acceleration". *Most* interesting.' The gratified smile on Winser's face slipped as the Doctor added kindly, 'Basic, mind you—but interesting. We must have a good long chat later on.' The Doctor waved a hand at the rows of dials. 'Now then, gentlemen ... As far as I can establish with these rather primitive instruments, the device or whatever has buried itself deep beneath the ground. That mound you saw represents the tip of the iceberg, so to speak. For the moment there's not much we can do about it.'

Jo saw Hardiman look meaningfully at Winser. Clearly he was wondering if this eccentric-looking character's conclusions could be relied upon. Winser stepped forward. 'Perhaps I could check your calculations, Doctor?'

For a moment the Doctor frowned. Jo held her breath, fearing an explosion. Then, to her relief, he gave one of his sudden charming smiles. 'Please do, my dear fellow.' He handed the clipboard to Winser. 'As you can see, the thing appears to be some kind of vehicle. Only there doesn't seem to be any trace of

life on board—not life in the conventional sense ...
Just listen to this.' The Doctor began adjusting the
controls. A deep throb, throb, throb, filled the
little control room, and a regular light-trace flashed
across a monitor screen.

Winser said slowly, 'It sounds like ...' His voice
trailed away as if he was unable to believe his own
thoughts.

'That's right,' said the Doctor. 'It sounds like a
giant heartbeat ...'

On the other side of the control room a head-
phoned technician said excitedly. 'There's something
coming through on the audio circuits. I'll put it on
full amplification.'

Seconds later a sibilant voice filled the air. 'Axos
calling Earth, Axos calling Earth ...' The whispering
voice was weak and erratic as if the speaker was using
the last of his energy. 'Fuel system exhausted ... request immediate assistance ... Axos calling ... request
assistance ...' The pleading voice faded away.

The Doctor rubbed his chin. 'Doesn't sound very
like a threat, does it? More of a call for help.'

Chinn grasped the Brigadier's arm. 'If they *are*
weak, Brigadier, now's the time to attack, before they
can organise their defences!'

The Doctor said, 'Before you have another go at
annihilating the thing, Brigadier, may I make a
suggestion?'

'Well, Doctor?'

'Why don't we just go and take a look at it?' The
Doctor made for the door. As Jo started to follow
him, he said, 'I'm sorry, Jo, not you.'

The Brigadier nodded. 'Quite agree. Captain Yates,

32

you will stay here as liaison officer. Look after Miss Grant. Sergeant Benton, you check the perimeter guard.'

The control room emptied rapidly as everyone began to leave. Chinn hung around indecisively, clearly reluctant to leave the safety of the control room. The Brigadier paused in the doorway. 'Well, Mr Chinn, aren't you going to join us? You are our Co-ordinator, you know.'

Reluctantly Chinn followed the Brigadier, and Jo was left alone with the technician and Mike Yates. Giving him an appealing smile, she started for the door. 'Mike, couldn't I just ...'

Yates stepped quickly in front of her. 'No you couldn't! You heard the Brigadier.'

Jo glared mutinously at him. If there was one thing she hated it was being looked after, particularly when there was something exciting going on. She was about to start arguing when Benton reappeared in the doorway. 'Sir, we've found a body!'

'Where?'

'In the trees, behind that mound thing. There's a car, too. Big American job.'

'All right, Sergeant. I'll come and take a look.'

As Jo started to follow them out of the control room, Benton stopped her. 'Better stay here, Miss Grant. It's not too pleasant to look at.'

Benton too, thought Jo indignantly. It was a conspiracy! She opened her mouth to protest—then closed it and sat meekly on a stool. 'All right, I'll wait here.'

Jo stayed on her stool just long enough to allow

Yates and Benton to get clear, then nipped smartly out of the door.

On the steps of the Mobile H.Q. she paused, looking around. Should she follow Yates and Benton and take a look at the mysterious corpse, or try to catch up with the Doctor and his party? Deciding that an alien spaceship was a bigger attraction than a dead body, Jo started running quickly towards the mound.

At the edge of the clump of trees Yates was gazing incredulously at the wizened body of a bearded old man. It lay on its back, stiff hands raised clawlike to fend off some approaching horror. But it was the *condition* of the body that was so extraordinary. It was dried up, completely mummified, as if it had lain for years under the desert sun. Yates knelt down and touched the leathery skin. To his horror the face crumbled away beneath his fingers ...

Not far away, on the other side of the mound, a heated argument was going on amongst the Doctor's group. Their inspection of the mound had revealed precisely nothing. Chinn wanted the thing bombed or at least shelled immediately, and for all his dislike of the man, the Brigadier tended to agree with him. Hardiman and Winser were opposed to this, fearing that such an attack might cause an explosion large enough to damage the Nuton Complex. The Doctor took no part in the debate. He stood staring absorbedly at the mound, running his hand along the strange gourd-like surface, wishing they'd all go away and let him take a really good look at it.

Suddenly the Doctor felt a violent throbbing. He jumped back as a space appeared before him. The hole grew and grew until it resembled an arched opening. Through it a glowing corridor led downwards, deep into the heart of the mound.

The little group was stunned. The Doctor was the first to recover. Waving a hand towards the opening he said cheerily, 'An open door, gentlemen—which presumably means an invitation to go in. Shall we take a look?'

Without waiting for their agreement, the Doctor stepped inside, and slowly the others followed. Jo Grant came running up just in time to see them all disappear through the opening. She hesitated for a moment. She'd wanted to *see* the mound, but she hadn't reckoned on going inside it. And suppose the door closed again? Deciding she'd better risk it, Jo dashed inside.

She found herself in a kind of tunnel, leading downwards, its walls aglow with light. Just ahead of her she could hear the voices of the others. Jo crept along quietly behind them, not wanting to be seen.

Ahead of her, the Doctor and his companions came to an archway. It seemed to lead into a large chamber. One by one they stepped through. The Doctor waited until last, watching as the others went by. He noticed that as each one stepped through the archway multi-coloured lights played over their faces and there was a faint crackle of energy. Clearly they were passing through some kind of scanning system. When the others were all through, the Doctor himself stepped under the archway. Immediately he felt his mind gripped by an immensely powerful force. It seemed to be trying to tear the knowledge from his brain. Strange lights and patterns whirled before his eyes, and he felt the tentacles of alien thought groping within his mind. Only with a mighty effort was he able to break free of their grip and force himself through the archway. Half-collapsing, he staggered into the chamber beyond.

(Deep inside Axos the Doctor's analysis pattern appeared on a screen before the glowing eye. The voice whispered, 'Analysis pattern indicates subject non-typical. High intelligence, possibly of extra-terrestrial origin. Investigate!')

The Doctor became aware that someone was holding him up and a blurred voice was speaking. 'Doctor, what's happened to you? Are you all right?' Suddenly everything came back into focus and he saw the worried face of the Brigadier. 'Thought you'd fainted for a moment,' said the Brigadier gruffly. 'Felt a bit dizzy myself going through that arch. Nothing like so bad as you, though ...'

The Doctor straightened up. 'I'm all right now. Full of surprises, this place.'

From the corridor, Jo Grant had watched the Doctor's struggle in the archway. Worried, she peeped through and saw him, apparently unharmed, talking to the Brigadier. Jo decided not to risk going through the arch. It seemed to hold some kind of alarm system which might detect her as an intruder. If she explored further down the corridor, perhaps she could steal a march on the others by discovering the secrets of this strange place before they did. That would teach them to try and keep her out of things! Jo crept cautiously on her way.

Meanwhile the Doctor and his companions were examining their surroundings. They were in a large oval chamber, walls, floor and ceiling all composed of the same strange glowing substance. They looked at each other in puzzlement. The chamber although impressive was completely empty. 'What do we do now?' whispered the Brigadier.

'Wait. We've been brought here for some reason ...' The Doctor pointed. 'Look, over there!'

On the far side of the chamber, part of the wall was becoming transparent. Light flooded from behind it, and they saw a group of figures standing in an alcove. The dividing wall simply melted away, and the figures could be seen more clearly. The group of visitors was frozen in sheer astonishment. None of them, not even the Doctor, had imagined anything like the creatures before them.

There were four of them. They were humanoid in appearance, and incredibly beautiful. They wore one-piece silvery garments of simple design, and their skins were a pale gleaming gold.

They seemed to be a family. There was a man, a woman, a boy and a girl. All four stood still for a moment, looking like golden statues. Then the man stepped forward and the others followed him. He held up his hand in greeting, and began to speak. His voice was clear, resonant, and hypnotically compelling. 'Our worlds are uncountable light-years away on the far rim of the galaxy. Our planetary system has been crippled by solar flare activity. By now, no doubt, all of our worlds are totally and permanently entropised.'

The Brigadier shot the Doctor an agonised glance of enquiry. The Doctor whispered, 'Drained of all life and energy!'

The Brigadier nodded his understanding. The golden man waved an expressive hand around him. 'We are the Axons. You stand in the heart of Axos, all that is left of our culture.'

Winser said incredulously, 'Then this *is* some kind of spaceship? You built it for your journey?'

The Axon shook his head. 'Not built. As you see our technology has taken a different path from yours. The ship was *grown*, from a single cell. Now its nutrient is all but exhausted. We should like to stay here, to replenish our energy and nutrition cycles. In return we offer you a gift ... a payment.' He lifted a hand and a low pedestal rose up before them. On it rested a small golden casket. The golden man said simply, 'Axonite!'

He lifted the lid and the visitors clustered round. Inside the casket lay a formless blob that shimmered and pulsed with light, like some exotic jewel. It blurred and shifted beneath their eyes.

The Axon smiled at their puzzlement. 'Axonite is the source of all our technology. Axonite can absorb, convert, transmit and programme all other forms of energy.'

'Even radiation?' said the Doctor suddenly. 'Even solar radiation?'

The Brigadier realised that the Doctor was pointing out an inconsistency in the Axon's story. With this wonder-working substance at their command, why hadn't the Axons been able to solve their own problems?

Sadly the Axon bowed his head. 'Axonite can only control energy that *exists*. By the time we realised our danger, it was already too late.'

Chinn glared reproachfully at the Doctor, indicating that his scepticism was in thoroughly bad taste. He turned back to the Axon. 'If you could explain what this substance is, what it does . . .'

'Axonite is the chameleon of the elements. It uses the energy it absorbs not only to copy but to restructure and re-create any given substance, if necessary improving on the original . . .'

Chinn looked thoroughly bewildered. Clearly the Axon's explanation left him no wiser.

The Doctor interrupted again. 'Yet you still ran out of fuel?'

Again the Axon bowed his head. 'The fault was ours. At the lowest ebb of our energy cycle, even Axonite cannot help us. There is no energy left with which it can work.'

Winser was studying the glowing substance. 'The principle?' he demanded. 'What is the principle of Axonite?'

'Axonite can be called a thinking molecule. Its subatomic particles behave in an ordered rather than a random manner. They can be programmed so that every molecule acts as a micro-computer, linked in turn to every other molecule . . .'

Beside him the Brigadier heard the Doctor whisper, 'Like a kind of brain . . .'

The Axon went on, 'Surely it would be simpler if I were to demonstrate Axonite? Then you may take this sample and examine it for yourselves.' He moved to the recess and took from it another casket. 'We have captured a small living creature of your planet.' The Axon put his hand inside the casket and took out a toad, placing it carefully on the floor in front of him.

The toad crouched motionless, looking around it with jewelled eyes. The Axon produced a transparent device rather like a large hypodermic. A blob of Axonite could be seen glowing somewhere inside it. He touched the toad gently on its glistening back. 'A painless lasonic injection ...'

The scene was at once mysterious and absurd, thought the Brigadier. There they all stood in the glowing heart of this mysterious space craft, confronting these golden-skinned, smooth-tongued Axons—and their pet toad!

Suddenly the toad began to grow. It grew and grew until it towered over them, transformed from a humble toad into a terrifying monster. They could see the pulsing of the enormous throat, the gleam of the huge eyes. The great mouth opened and the long tongue flicked out ... Chinn screamed and scrambled backwards, cannoning into the rest of them ...

The Axon touched the monster's back with his device. 'The process is, of course, reversible.' The monster began to shrink, dwindling with incredible speed until it was once more a harmless toad, blinking up at them. The Axon lifted it carefully and returned it to its casket.

'If this had been one of your food animals ... I am sure you can see the possibilities for alleviating your world food problems.'

The Brigadier had a sudden staggering vision of cattle as big as houses, pigs like giant barrage-balloons. He shook his head to clear it, and heard the Doctor asking another of his awkward questions. 'Does this process also apply to inorganic materials? To fissionable material?'

The Axon nodded gravely. 'With certain necessary adaptations.'

Winser grabbed Hardiman's arm in a painful grip and whispered, 'We *must* have it. Whatever they want give it to them! We *must* have Axonite!'

Chinn scrambled to his feet and tried to regain his composure. He managed to address the Axon in something like his usual pompous tones. 'If the British Government is to consent to this arrangement, an agreement will have to be properly negotiated ...'

The Doctor's voice cut across Chinn's flow of words. 'Do you really believe this substance is going to benefit you? Your world should be allowed to develop at its own pace ...'

Winser whispered fiercely, 'We are being offered the greatest scientific discovery since—since atomic energy.'

'Exactly. And look at the use you made of that! It was touch and go whether you annihilated yourselves ...'

Chinn came to Winser's support. 'Brigadier, I must insist you silence this man. He is jeopardising vital negotiations ...'

But the Brigadier had reached some conclusions of his own. 'Mr Chinn, if this material leaves this spaceship, it will do so in my possession. This is a matter for the entire United Nations. The consequences are of international importance and the U.N. will decide ...'

Chinn waved a dismissive hand. 'This ship is on British soil, and the offer made by our friends here ...'

The clear voice of the Axon cut across their

wrangling. 'Since there is so much disagreement amongst so few—what of the whole planet? We shall withdraw and give you time to decide ...'

Followed by his family the Axon stepped back into the recess. The children disappeared through a small door. The Axon man and woman stood patiently waiting. For a moment there was silence. Then the arguments broke out with renewed force ...

Jo Grant moved slowly along the glowing corridor. It seemed to go on endlessly, winding to and fro so that she soon lost all sense of direction. Panic-stricken she decided to go back and find the others. She turned and ran the way she had come. Suddenly she heard a voice, faint but clear. It was a man's voice and there was an edge of panic to it. 'Help, help,' it was calling. 'Somebody get me out of here.'

Despite the faintness, Jo recognised the voice immediately. It was Bill Filer. She remembered Benton's message just before she left the Mobile H.Q. Something about a body—and an American car ... Jo guessed at once what must have happened. Filer had got here before them, and somehow he'd been captured. She moved in the direction of the voice, calling, 'Filer? Mr Filer, where are you?'

The faint voice seemed to vibrate along the glowing walls. 'Help ... help ...' Then it faded away.

Jo called again, 'Mr Filer! Can you hear me?'

This time there was no reply and she hammered her fist angrily against the wall. Behind her, the opposite wall of the corridor began to bulge outwards. The bulge was about the size and shape of a man.

But the shape that emerged from it was no more than a ghastly parody of a man, a shambling shapeless creature that seemed made up of hundreds of squirming tentacles ...

Alarmed by a sudden rustling noise, Jo swung round. She screamed as the quivering horror advanced towards her ...

4

Enter the Master

Bill Filer awoke, his mind still full of the horror of the great glowing eye. He thought he'd been having a bad dream till the restraining pressure of the tentacles told him the nightmare was ghastly reality. For a moment he panicked. 'Help! Help!' he yelled. 'Somebody get me out of here!' For a moment he actually thought he heard a reply, someone calling his name. 'Help! Help!' he yelled again.

'You're wasting your time, my friend.'

Filer looked round wildly. Fully awake at last, he realised that this place of imprisonment had changed. He was in a small enclosed space, a glowing-walled cell. Tentacles growing from walls and floor held him firmly in place. On the other side of the cell, more tentacles were securing another prisoner. Filer looked curiously at him. The man wore a dark suit, with a high-collared jacket. Although he wasn't particularly big, his compact body gave an impression of immense power. He had a small, neatly-pointed black beard and dark burning eyes. His voice was deep and resonant. 'Who are you? What is your name?'

So compelling was the voice that Filer answered without question. 'Bill Filer. American Intelligence.' He gazed bemusedly at the other man. Surely his appearance was familiar. No, not his appearance. His *description*. Filer struggled to regain his concentration. 'And who the hell are you?'

The bearded man smiled ironically. 'At the moment I am simply your fellow captive, Filer. In more fortunate circumstances, I am known as the Master!'

Although Jo didn't realise it, she was now very close to the chamber where she'd left the others. The sound of her terrified screams broke up their heated discussion.

The Doctor dashed out of the chamber and along the corridor, the Brigadier close behind. Hardiman and Winser were about to follow when Chinn gestured them to remain. He turned to the Axon. 'Now perhaps we can talk without perpetual interference from UNIT. About this agreement ...'

The Axon was not listening. He had pressed his hand to a section of wall which seemed to grow brighter at his touch. He stood for a moment as if communing with the very fabric of the ship, then said politely. 'I'm afraid there is some crisis. I must investigate.'

'Then perhaps you would escort me from your ship? Discreetly as possible. I must get in touch with my Minister.'

'Of course.' The Axon gestured towards the Axon woman. She indicated that Chinn should follow her, and led him towards the small door. The Axon hurried out after the Doctor. Hardiman and Winser were left gazing helplessly at each other.

After a moment Hardiman said doubtfully, 'Winser, are you sure ...'

'I'm sure that Axonite offers the greatest potential for scientific advancement we've ever known.' There was a fanatical light in Winser's eyes. 'It ties in with my own research with the Particle Accelerator—immeasurably more advanced, of course. We must have Axonite, here in the Nuton laboratories. Whatever the cost ...'

The Doctor found Jo crumpled on the floor in a dead faint. Standing over her was the golden figure of an Axon. For a moment the Doctor thought that the Axon he'd left in the chamber had somehow arrived ahead of him, since the appearance was identical. Same inhumanly handsome features, same pale golden skin.

The Axon backed slowly away as the Doctor ran up. He didn't speak as the Doctor knelt by Jo and examined her. She was already recovering. After a moment she opened her eyes and said dazedly, 'Doctor?'

'It's all right, Jo, you're safe now. What happened?'

'I saw this thing ... this monster. It was all slimy and tentacled ...' Jo's voice began rising in panic.

'Jo—it's all right. There's nothing to be afraid of.' The Doctor helped Jo to get to her feet.

Masking his concern with abruptness, the Brigadier said, 'May I ask what you're doing here, Miss Grant? I gave you explicit orders.'

'I know. I'm afraid I followed you in. Then I heard Bill Filer's voice ...'

'*Filer*—in here?'

'I tried to find him ... then this awful thing appeared. It came right out of the wall at me ...'

The Axon they had first encountered, presumably their leader, thought the Brigadier, came quietly up to them. He looked at his fellow Axon for a moment. Without a word the Axon turned and walked away. Calmly the Axon leader said, 'I think I can explain. We are close to the organic power-sources here. Emission from the energy cells, weak as it is, might still have affected your sense perceptions, causing you to hallucinate.'

'What about the voice I heard?'

The Doctor patted her shoulder. 'All part of the hallucination, Jo.' he said reassuringly. 'Even I was affected when I first came in. Let's go back to the others.'

In a small communications booth inside the Mobile H.Q., Chinn stood impatiently waiting as the UNIT R/T Operator linked him up with Whitehall. When at last the call was through Chinn said abruptly. 'Just wait outside, will you?'

'Sir?'

'Wait outside!'

The R/T Operator looked doubtful, but he knew Chinn was some kind of VIP. He said woodenly. 'Very good, sir,' and left Chinn alone in the little booth. The Minister's face appeared on the monitor screen. He looked rather like a cunning old bloodhound. Chinn poured out his story, careful to emphasise the immense potential value of Axonite and the obstructive attitude taken by the Brigadier and his eccentric Scientific Adviser. He explained his plan for dealing with them, and secured the Minister's permission to assume special powers. But the Minister's final words were far from encouraging.

'You're *sure* you can handle this, Chinn?'

'With the special powers I've requested, yes, sir.'

'Because if you're not, remember this. It's your head on the block, Chinn, not mine.' With a certain relish in his voice the Minister went on, 'If anything *should* go awry, Chinn, your reputation, indeed your whole career will be ruined. You will bear that in mind, won't you?'

Chinn gulped. 'Yes, sir.'

'Remember Chinn, no one is indispensable—except me, of course.'

'Quite sir. About the special powers ...'

'I'll get in touch with the Regulars right away.' The Minister was unable to resist a final jibe. 'Just keep me informed, won't you? Remember, you're the man on the spot—in more ways than one!' The Minister smiled appreciatively at his own joke, then the screen went dark.

Chinn looked at his watch. 'Right, Brigadier,' he thought. 'Now we'll see where the *real* power lies ...'

The Axon was concluding a polished speech of apology. 'Naturally I regret that your young female was frightened. But to wander about our ship was a rash thing to do. Of course, if Miss Grant would like to see over the ship, we shall be happy for her to do so. Under the proper supervision, that is ...'

It was all very smooth and convincing, thought

Jo. Too convincing. She tugged at the Doctor's sleeve and whispered, 'Doctor, I *did* see that creature. And I *did* hear Filer's voice. It wasn't an hallucination. It was real.'

The Doctor said loudly, 'The whole point about hallucinations is that people do think they're real. Otherwise they wouldn't be hallucinations, would they?'

Jo subsided, with a distinct feeling that the Doctor was letting her down.

The Doctor strolled across to Hardiman and Winser, who were studying the specimen of Axonite in its golden casket. Winser nodded towards Jo. 'No ill effects?'

The Doctor shook his head. 'She'll be all right.'

The Axon moved towards the door in the recess. 'I will leave you, gentlemen. Until the question is settled.'

The Doctor watched the Axon go and then asked breezily, 'What question?'

Winser tapped the casket. 'Axonite. Chinn's gone to talk to his Minister.'

The Doctor thought hard. It was easy to deduce Chinn's next move—which meant he must make some readjustments of his own. He smiled at Winser. 'Beware of the Greeks bearing gifts.'

'What?'

'You're referring to the story of the Trojan Horse, Doctor?' said Hardiman. The Doctor nodded.

Jo was listening to the conversation in some puzzlement. She remembered the story of the Trojan horse from her schooldays. The Greeks had been besieging Troy, and couldn't get inside. So they'd built an

49

enormous wooden horse, left it outside the city gates and gone away. Overcome with curiosity, the Trojans had dragged the horse inside their city walls. But the horse had been hollow—and filled with Greek soldiers ... She couldn't quite see how this applied to Axonite.

Neither could Winser. 'These classical allusions are lost on me, Doctor. I'm a scientist.'

'So were the Greeks in their way. Unfortunately for Troy. Pretty little place it was. I used to have a villa there, right on the sea's edge. You could lie in bed and fish for your breakfast—before the Greeks destroyed the place of course ...' The Doctor became aware that Hardiman and Winser were staring at him in utter bafflement, and realised that his free and easy attitude to Time was causing some confusion. Hurriedly he said, 'Still, no use dwelling in the past, eh? We must look to the future.'

Hardiman seized his opportunity. 'And the future of humanity can benefit enormously from Axonite.'

'The advantages will be enormous ...' agreed Winser.

'The material advantages, perhaps.' The Doctor took the casket from Winser's hands and looked at the pulsating substance within. 'I doubt if even Axonite can increase the growth-rate of human common sense.' He shut the lid of the casket with a bang. 'However, since everyone is clearly hell-bent on getting hold of it, may I suggest that we confine it initially to your own labs? At least until we can make a proper analysis of all its properties?'

Hardiman seized on the key word. 'We? Are you offering to co-operate with us, Doctor?'

'Scientifically, yes.'

Hardiman looked at his colleague. 'Winser?'

'That depends.'

'On what?'

'On who is to lead the investigation.'

Hurriedly the Doctor said, 'Why you do, of course. My contribution would remain completely anonymous. Security reasons, you see.'

Winser smiled, thinking of the articles in scientific publications, the conferences, the books, even the Nobel Prize ...

'That fellow Chinn's the problem,' muttered Winser.

'What's he up to, Doctor?' asked Hardiman.

'I'm not sure. But believe me, Sir George, the longer we scientists can keep Axonite away from people like Chinn, the better for all of us.' The Doctor smiled cheerfully at his new allies.

Jo sidled up to him. 'Doctor, what are you up to? What about the Brigadier? What about the United Nations? You're supposed to be working for UNIT.'

'I wish you wouldn't keep interrupting, Jo. These matters are rather above your head.' Ignoring her stricken face, the Doctor turned to Winser. 'Do tell me more about your Particle Accelerator. I gather you've reached a g-factor of point eight? A remarkable achievement!'

Winser smiled, pleased that this odd-looking fellow appreciated the value of his work. His smile vanished when the Doctor added, 'And I imagine that with a factor of say, one point one, you hope to be able to travel in Time?'

Winser was astonished. The eventual aims of his

research had been carefully concealed, yet the Doctor had deduced them with casual ease. Hurriedly revising his estimate of the Doctor's intelligence Winser said quietly, 'Well, in theory ...'

'But only if the reaction is controllable. With Axonite perhaps?'

Winser looked hard at him. 'Why not? Clearly Axonite must have an existence in the fourth dimension ... That being the case ...'

The rest of the conversation was over Jo's head, but she scarcely bothered to listen. Her mind was full of a shocking discovery. Now she knew why the Doctor had suddenly changed his attitude. He didn't care whether Axonite would be good or bad for Humanity. He wanted it for himself!

With wriggling and twisting that would have done credit to a professional acrobat, Bill Filer had managed to manoeuvre his Colt Cobra from his shoulder holster into his hand. Taking careful aim he fired at one of the tentacles holding him captive. His second bullet severed one tentacle, but the others tightened their grip.

'That won't help you, Filer.'

Filer said nothing. He knew the Master was right. Even if he scored a hit every time—which he wouldn't —there were still too many tentacles and too few bullets. Persuasively the Master continued, 'If you'll only listen to me, we can both escape.'

'Oh, sure.' Filer gave a scowl of frustration. Here he was just a few feet from the man he'd been hunting—and he couldn't do a thing about it.

The Master went on talking. Despite himself Filer found his attention caught and held by the deep, persuasive voice. 'Listen, Filer! We are both prisoners of Axos. Whatever our differences we *must* join forces.'

'What *is* Axos? Where do they come from?'

'Nowhere.'

Filer said stubbornly. 'Everything's gotta come from somewhere.'

'No, Filer. The Axons have no home planet. If you like, this ship is their planet. They float in space, searching for food, for *energy*. They are scavengers of the universe ...'

'So how come they chose Earth? Did you bring them here?'

'I had no choice. They captured me, absorbed me. They forced me to bring them to a living planet. It was the price of my freedom. And then they tricked me. If you don't help me, Filer, this whole world, your world, will be doomed.'

Filer considered. 'O.K. I can't get in any worse mess. What do I do?'

'You see that small nodule, high up in the wall? It is the nerve centre of this cell. If you can hit it, the shock will disorientate it, at least temporarily.'

'And that'll give us our chance?'

'Our only chance!'

Filer looked doubtfully at the tiny projection. He was a fine pistol shot, and under normal conditions he would have felt pretty confident. But conditions were anything but normal. Trussed hand and foot, in poor light, he would have to shoot at a half-seen target with his hand stretched awkwardly across his body. Taking the best aim he could, he fired. A tiny hole appeared at the edge of the nodule. Filer looked at the Master. 'So? Nothing happened.'

'You must hit the centre, Filer. The *exact* centre.'

Filer fired again—and again. The shots were close —but not close enough. He looked at the Master. 'Last chance!' Taking careful aim, he squeezed the trigger with agonising slowness. The revolver cracked —and a hole appeared in the very centre of the nodule.

Immediately there was chaos. The tentacles loosened their grip and lashed aimlessly about. Lights flickered madly and even the walls and floor seemed to ripple with shock. The Master gripped the inter-twined tendrils that formed one wall and ripped them apart. When the gap was big enough, they forced their way through it and tore off down the corridor.

Jo was still trying to convince the Brigadier of the Doctor's treachery. 'You know how obsessed he is with getting the TARDIS going again? Well, he's talk-ing Time Travel with Winser. He's got the idea that Axonite will help him to get away from Earth.'

The Brigadier looked doubtful. It was true enough that escape from Earth in the TARDIS was the Doc-tor's prime concern. He'd only taken the job with UNIT in return for laboratory facilities to work on his TARDIS. Even so, he'd given valuable help in the past and the Brigadier found it hard to accept that his old friend was planning to betray him. Worriedly he said, 'Keep an eye on the Doctor by all means, Miss Grant. It's Chinn I'm worried about. He's been away for ages now. What's *he* up to?'

As if on cue Chinn bustled back into the chamber, the Axon leader beside him. Chinn was in high spirits. 'It's all over, Brigadier. I've reached full agreement with our friend here.'

The Brigadier realised that he'd been outflanked. Chinn had been back in the Axon ship for some time —engaged in a private conference with the Axon leader. Importantly Chinn went on, 'Britain now has the world rights to Axonite.' He took the casket from Winser and tucked it possessively under his arm.

The Brigadier's voice was cold. 'You leave me no alternative, Mr Chinn.' He drew his revolver and levelled it at the astonished civil servant. 'I'll take charge of that.' Taking the casket from Chinn the Brigadier gestured with the revolver. 'Now then everyone—shall we go?'

Herding Chinn ahead of him, the Brigadier led them from the chamber. The Axon stood silently watching, making no attempt to stop them. When he stood alone in the chamber a sibilant voice filled the air.

'Energy crisis in cell area. Investigate.'

The Axon turned to leave. Before he did so he spoke to the Axon woman. 'Further personalisation unnecessary. Commence reabsorption.' He hurried away.

The beautiful golden-skinned woman stepped back against the wall. Her beauty dissolved into a mass of writhing tentacles which in turn merged into the wall of the ship. Now she was once more part of Axos.

The journey back to the Mobile H.Q. was made in an awkward silence, everyone preoccupied by their own thoughts. Chinn appeared suspiciously cheerful for someone who'd just suffered a major defeat.

The Brigadier waved his party into the Mobile H.Q. At the top of the steps, he stopped in astonishment. The control room was full of armed soldiers. Yates and Benton stood stiffly to attention covered by a corporal's sten-gun. A Regular Army Captain was standing by Chinn's side.

The Brigadier exploded. 'Yates, Benton, what the blazes is going on here?'

It was Yates who replied. 'Regulars just moved in and took over, sir.'

'Took over?'

Benton nodded sheepishly. 'Took us all by surprise, sir. I mean—we couldn't very well open fire.'

'What about the rest of the men?'

This time it was Chinn who answered the question. 'They have all been arrested.'

With a sudden movement he snatched the golden casket from under the Brigadier's arm. 'And so, Brigadier, have you.'

5

The Doctor Makes a Plan

For a moment the Brigadier was literally speechless with rage. There was a tense silence in the crowded control room. Then, in a voice choked with anger, he began, 'You have no *right* ...' He moved to recover the casket, only to find one of the soldiers barring his way with a levelled sten-gun.

Chinn smiled triumphantly. 'On the contrary, I have every right, Brigadier. You and your people are all under arrest. I have been granted special powers by the Minister.'

Ignoring Chinn, the Brigadier snapped, 'I must warn you, Captain ...?'

'Harker, sir.'

'... Captain Harker, that this is an illegal act.'

'I'm sorry, sir. I must follow my orders.'

The Brigadier nodded, understanding his fellow-soldier's discomfort. 'Very well. Mr Chinn, I submit under protest. I shall make every attempt to inform the U.N.'

'Thank you for the warning, Brigadier. Captain Harker, I want these men under twenty-four hour armed guard, inside the Complex. They are to communicate with no one, you understand? *No one!* If you need me I shall be at the Nuton Complex myself.'

Chinn, Hardiman and Winser left. Seconds later,

came the sound of their car driving off. Captain Harker moved over to the Brigadier. 'I must ask for your weapon, sir.'

Slowly the Brigadier drew his service revolver and handed it over.

'Thank you, sir. Now, if you'll all come with me?'

The Brigadier, Yates and Benton were escorted from the room by the soldiers. The Captain waited, looking enquiringly at the Doctor and Jo, who hadn't moved.

Almost absent-mindedly, the Doctor waved him away. 'Your orders don't apply to us, young man. We're both civilians, aren't we, Jo?'

Jo nodded, although actually they were nothing of the sort. They were both members of UNIT, and she was quite sure that Chinn had intended them to be arrested with the others.

Harker looked worried. 'I shall have to check with Mr Chinn, sir.'

'Then do so. Now if you don't mind, we have important work to do.' The Doctor began leafing through a pile of reports.

Captain Harker hesitated. There was something very impressive about the Doctor's air of casual authority. He was already unhappy about his orders, and he certainly didn't want to exceed them. 'Very well, sir. You can stay here for the time being. I should warn you that all communications are in the hands of my own men and there are armed guards outside.'

Totally absorbed in his reports, the Doctor didn't seem to hear him. Harker paused, then went out of the control room.

The Doctor looked up at Jo and grinned. 'For a while, I didn't think it was going to work.'

'Well it *won't* work, not for long. As soon as he checks with Chinn, we'll be locked up with the others.'

'Never mind. We've gained a little time and we must make good use of it. Now, tell me everything that happened to you in the Axon ship. I want to know more about this creature you saw. And are you certain you heard Bill Filer?'

'You mean you *believe* me?'

The Doctor looked hurt. 'Of course I do, Jo. I believed you all the time.'

Filer and the Master didn't enjoy their freedom for very long. As they dashed down a corridor they found the golden form of the Axon leader waiting for them. Tentacles sprang out from the walls and held them in a remorseless grip. More Axons appeared and surrounded them.

The Master became very angry. 'I demand that you set me free. I have kept my part of the bargain. I insist ...'

'Silence!' There was such concentrated malignancy in the Axon leader's voice that even the Master was quelled. 'Take the human away.'

The tentacles holding Filer loosened their grip, and two Axons began dragging him away. He struggled wildly but the Axons had inhuman strength. 'What's going on?' he yelled. 'Where are you taking me?'

Surprisingly the Axon leader answered him. 'To the replication section.'

The Master watched dispassionately as his fellow prisoner was dragged away. 'Goodbye, Filer. I don't think we shall be meeting again.'

The Axon leader turned to his helpers. 'Take the Time Lord back to his cell.' Remorselessly, the golden figures closed in on the Master.

Jo finished her story and looked up at the Doctor.

'What's going on, Doctor? What *is* Axonite, really?'

'Beads and tinsel for fools and savages . . . and something more. Why should they foist this gift on Earth? What do they want?' The Doctor frowned. 'Frankly, Jo, I find myself in something of a quandry.'

Jo remembered the Doctor's conversation with Winser, the interest he'd shown in the possible applications of Axonite to Time travel, 'About which side you're on? For a while I thought you were changing sides.'

The Doctor seemed determined to change the subject. He tapped the pile of UNIT reports. 'What about this car they found? And the body?'

Jo shrugged. 'The car was Filer's all right. The body disintegrated when they touched it.'

'So it could have been Filer?'

'No! I tell you I heard him. He's still alive, inside the Axon ship.'

'I only hope you're right, Jo.'

'I tell you he's in there. And we've got to get him out. We'll make the Axons let us search the ship.'

A familiar, hated voice spoke out. 'You will do no such thing.' Chinn was in the doorway, Winser and

Captain Harker by his side. He marched up to Jo and said angrily, 'There will be no search. As far as I am concerned, the man Filer has ceased to exist.'

Struggling against restraining tentacles, Filer was once more a helpless captive, this time in another part of the Axon ship. He sensed he was somewhere close to the power sources. The walls glowed more brightly, and a deep throbbing filled the air. Bright multi-coloured lights flashed before his eyes, and waves of dizziness swept over him.

Dimly Filer became aware that something was happening to the wall opposite him. A long bulge was forming, swelling out ... A bulge about the size and shape of a man. Filer struggled wildly as the bulge became a writhing many-tentacled monster. It changed again into the familiar golden form of an Axon. Then the creature began a third and final change, and Filer's eyes widened in horror at the unbelievable sight before him ... He was looking at himself.

Jo used every argument she could think of to persuade Chinn to search for Filer. But she soon realised she was wasting her time—Chinn simply refused to listen. Finally she turned away in disgust. 'All you care about, Mr Chinn, is your contemptible underhand deal with the Axons!'

'That agreement is vitally important, young lady, and I will allow nothing to prejudice its success. This man Filer is not going to cause an unpleasant incident. There will be no search. The man is expendable and that is that!' Chinn paused for breath. 'Captain Harker, have them both taken to the Complex and put them with the Brigadier. Remember, they are to be held incommunicado—no contact with anyone.'

Suddenly Winser said, 'Take the girl by all means. But not the Doctor. He's going to help me with the preliminary investigations of Axonite.'

Chinn thought for a moment. 'Very well. But remember this, Doctor. The slightest hint of sabotage or delay—and it's your head on the block, not mine.'

The Doctor ignored him, and turned to Winser. 'After you, my dear fellow. I can't wait to begin our collaboration.'

As Winser and the Doctor moved off, Jo said sadly, 'So you *have* changed sides after all, Doctor?'

The Doctor paused in the doorway, and gave her a benign smile. 'A matter of basic loyalties, my dear. I'm afraid mine must always be to science.'

The Master looked up as the golden figure of the Axon leader entered the cell. 'Well? *Am* I to be released?'

'Perhaps. This indeed is a rich planet you have brought us to.'

'Then set me free!'

'In due course. As yet we have only gained a foothold on this planet. For us to achieve the maximum nutrient value, Axonite must encircle this world within the next seventy-two Earth hours ...'

'And something's gone wrong?' The Master looked

keenly at his captor, sensing that there was a reason behind this visit.

Briefly the Axon told of the agreement reached with Chinn. 'We were forced to accept his terms. The Doctor and the Brigadier were suspicious. They might have refused to accept Axonite. The greed of the human called Chinn blinded him to all dangers.'

The Master laughed scornfully. 'And now your hands are tied. For Axonite to be distributed word-wide this secret agreement must be broken. I can do that for you—*if* you give me my freedom. We made a bargain ...'

'But the contract is not yet completed. The bargain, you remember, was that if we spared you and your TARDIS, you would lead us to this planet.'

'As I have done!' The Master's voice was savage. 'And you made me a further promise. The death of the Doctor—and the destruction of all life on this miserable planet.'

'Of course. But when this Doctor visited our ship, our sensors detected something you failed to tell us. The Doctor is also a Time Lord, is he not?'

Two more Axons carried the unconscious body of Filer into the cell, and flung it into a corner.

The Axon raised a hand and the tentacles holding the Master relaxed their grip. 'Come. You may explain your plan. But remember—no one is irreplaceable.'

The Doctor stood looking round Winser's laboratory, a fixed expression of admiration on his face. Privately he was thinking that Winser's equipment was both

63

primitive and clumsy. But it might serve his purpose. A plan was beginning to form in the Doctor's mind . . .

Dominating the enormous laboratory was Winser's pride and joy—the Particle Accelerator. It was a complicated piece of equipment resembling in appearance a massive electronic cannon. In the centre of the 'barrel' section was a transparent door, made of heavy-duty plastic, and just in front of the giant machine stood a three-sided control panel.

The Doctor glanced casually around the huge circular room, taking his bearings. It was rather like being on the inside of a vast pottery kiln. An iron staircase led to a viewing gallery, and just above the gallery was the main control room. A huge picture window looked from it onto the laboratory. The Doctor could see Chinn peering suspiciously down at him, Hardiman at his side. The laboratory was in a separate wing, and the Doctor knew that there were armed soldiers outside. Chinn wasn't taking any chances with his precious Axonite. The golden casket stood on a laboratory bench nearby.

The Doctor walked round the Particle Accelerator, his mind rapidly absorbing Winser's explanations. Winser touched a massive lever. 'These subcontrols are linked to those in the main control-room up there—*this* lever brings in the entire output of Reactor One.'

The Doctor nodded. 'And with that colossal surge of power you accelerate the particles in an ever-increasing electromagnetic field?'

Winser nodded, surprised at how quickly the Doctor had grasped the purpose and function of the complex machinery. 'Precisely. Eventually I expect to achieve controlled acceleration up to and *beyond* the speed of light.' There was a fanatical gleam in Winser's eyes and his voice was hushed. 'Once beyond that, the particles will be travelling in the fourth dimension ... and I shall begin my experiments into the nature of Time itself.'

'With the ultimate aim of achieving Time travel?'

Winser nodded eagerly, relieved to find a fellow scientist who didn't think his theories too wild even to discuss. 'Why not?'

'Why not indeed?' The Doctor beamed at him. 'Well, it's all most impressive. Much larger than my own set-up of course,' he added casually. 'Mine's only about the size of ... well, say a police box.'

'Your set up? You mean to tell me you've already been working with ...'

'With a Time machine? Oh yes, very successfully too, for a while. Then I ran into some snags.'

The snags to which the Doctor referred were the laws of his own people, the Time Lords. As part of his sentence of exile to Earth, they had somehow prevented the TARDIS from functioning. In addition, they had clouded that part of the Doctor's memory that held the vital Temporal Equations, so that he was unable to repair it. But the Doctor was still determined to outwit them. Perhaps, in conjunction with Winser, he could somehow re-discover the information he needed. He sighed theatrically. 'Bit of a lash-up, the old TARDIS. But it functioned. I wish you could have seen it when it was working ...'

Winser was still grappling with the Doctor's extraordinary claim. 'Why have I never heard of this research? You've published nothing?'

'Er, no. Well, not in England, anyway.'

'Where then?'

'Oh, elsewhere. You see, old chap, I had a sort of breakdown. Believe me, afterwards I was a changed man! There are quite a few things I still can't remember.'

'How convenient!'

The Doctor shook his head. 'Most inconvenient, actually.' A sudden thought seemed to strike him. 'Still if you'd be interested in having a look at the old TARDIS, perhaps we could have it brought down?'

Winser gave him a puzzled look. 'Are you really serious about all this?'

The Doctor put a friendly hand on Winser's shoulder. 'Quite serious, I assure you. We could swop a few ideas ... cannibalise a few parts. Perhaps even get the old TARDIS operational.' He crossed to the laboratory bench and put his hand on the lid of the golden casket. 'Now we've got this stuff—we might as well make good use of it!'

The Master walked into the brain area of Axos, then stopped short in astonishment. Before the great eye on its flexible stalk stood a familiar figure. Filer! Not the exhausted, broken figure he had last seen but a new Filer, fresh and alert. The whispering voice of Axos filled the air around them.

'The other Time Lord will be with the Axonite. You will find him and bring him here.'

The Axon with the face and body of Filer nodded stiffly and walked away.

6

Escape from Axos

'No, Doctor! I simply won't hear of it!'

The Doctor groaned. His collaboration with Winser was getting off to a very poor start. The trouble was that Winser, being a careful and logical man, liked to carry out his experiments in a succession of careful and logical steps. The Doctor on the other hand favoured a more empirical approach—or as he himself expressed it, 'try it and see'. It was this attitude that was drawing such anguished protests from Winser. The Doctor stood by the Particle Accelerator, the golden casket in his hand.

'All we do is put the Axonite in here and whizz it about until we crack it down into particles!'

Winser was horrified. 'Far too dangerous. The whole lot could blow up.'

'But don't you see, it's the simplest way to break the Axonite down.'

'Doctor, if you think I'm going to risk fifty million pounds worth of equipment ... And how would we analyse the results?'

'If Axonite *is* a "thinking molecule", it should analyse itself. All we have to do is link up with the computer and read the print-out!'

'Analyse itself, indeed.' Winser beckoned a hovering assistant. 'That spectroscope set up yet?'

The assistant nodded, so intimidated by the row

that he scarcely dared speak. Winser took the casket from the Doctor and marched to the far corner of the laboratory.

The Doctor watched him in disgust. 'Spectroscope,' he muttered. 'You might just as well look at it through a very large magnifying glass!'

Winser turned. 'What was that, Doctor?'

'Oh nothing, my dear fellow. Just coming!'

Muttering 'Pompous ass,' (but well under his breath this time) the Doctor followed Winser across the lab.

Filer awoke slowly, his mind in a whirl of panic. Golden men and tentacled monsters had been bad enough. But seeing one of the Axon monsters turning into a copy of himself had been almost too much. Now Filer knew he had to escape. The Axons had created his replica for some purpose of their own—and whatever it was, he had to stop them.

Filer looked round. He was back in the cell area, alone this time. Tentacles were holding him—but their grip was slack and weak. He moved, and the tentacles tightened. Filer lay very still, thinking hard. Clearly the tentacles were activated by movement. The more he struggled the tighter they would grip. So if he moved very, very slowly ... Cautiously, inch by inch, Filer began edging towards the cell exit.

The Master stood in the Brain area, scrutinised by the Eye of Axos. He was pleading for his freedom with all the force at his command. 'I know the ways of the humans,' he urged. 'I can move freely, I am familiar with their organisations, their system. You do not have time to learn these things. If your Nutrition Cycle is to be activated within the next seventy-two hours, you must have world-wide distribution of Axonite.'

Behind the eye a part of the wall became a screen. Light-patterns flowed across it as the computer-like Brain of Axos considered and checked the Master's arguments. Then the Voice said, 'Data confirms feasibility of alien's plan. Motivation questionable. Decision ... release Time Lord but retain Time Capsule until successful completion of mission.'

The Master cursed silently. The Brain had guessed his intentions all too well. Once free of Axos he had planned to make one further attempt to kill the Doctor and then leave Earth, leaving the Axons to succeed or fail on their own. Now he was trapped, committed to helping the Axons as he had promised. As if to taunt him, a far recess of the Brain area lit up, revealing a plain white dome—about the size of a police box. It was the Master's TARDIS, in its basic, uncamouflaged form. He looked longingly towards it.

'I must have my TARDIS. Give it back to me.'

There was a mocking tone in the sibilant Voice. 'Negative. The Time Capsule is not needed for success of mission.'

'At least return my laser-pistol. I may need to defend myself.'

'Return of weapon is acceptable. Retention of Time Capsule will prevent hostile action.'

The Axon leader produced a stubby laser-pistol and handed it to the Master, who concealed it beneath his coat. 'Come,' he ordered, and led the Master away.

Filer walked very slowly, very calmly along the corridors of Axos, trying to find his way to some kind of exit. His every instinct screamed at him to run at top speed, but logic told him that this would trigger off Axon alarm systems. Step by step, he made his way, pausing only when he saw movement at a corridor junction. It was the Master, the Axon leader beside him. Keeping a safe distance, Filer began to follow them.

They led him through the maze of corridors, pausing at last in one which ended in a blank wall. The Axon raised his hand and a door slid back revealing a gleam of light. With a surge of hope, Filer realised they had reached an exit. The Master moved through the door. It began to close behind him ...

Filer broke into a run. He hurtled down the short corridor, flashed by the astonished Axon leader and threw himself through the rapidly closing gap. Behind him he heard the sudden clamour of the Axon alarms.

The Master was already running towards the clump of trees. An armed sentry appeared before him. 'Halt!'

Immediately the Master collapsed, gasping, 'I escaped ... they were keeping me prisoner ...'

As the sentry leaned over to help the Master to his feet, the Master smashed him to the ground with one savage blow. He ran quickly away into the trees.

A few minutes later, Filer came across the unconscious body of the sentry, and guessed it was the work of the Master. Filer drew his gun and reloaded it, then set off for the Nuton Complex at a run.

The Doctor and Winser examined the blob of Axonite as it sat smugly within its casket. They had subjected it to every imaginable laboratory test, and come up with precisely nothing. Winser slammed his fist down on the bench. 'Dammit, it must show *some* response to *something*.'

The Doctor shook his head. 'It's programmed not to. It's deliberately *resisting* analysis.'

Winser regarded him bitterly. 'Well go on—say, "I told you so".'

'I told you so,' repeated the Doctor obligingly. 'Now perhaps you'll listen. Particle acceleration is the only answer. Break it down and force it to analyse itself!'

'No. I won't risk my equipment.'

'Then will you risk mine?'

'I thought you said this ... TARDIS wasn't working.'

'Ah well—there is a certain malfunction in the drive system, but the rest is all right. If we could link through to the reactor and bypass the malfunction ...'

Winser began to look more hopeful. 'If your equipment is compatible with my Particle Accelerator ... it *might* work ...'

And so might the TARDIS, thought the Doctor, though he didn't say so aloud. 'Well, it's worth a try, isn't it? After all, what else is there left to use? Now if you can convince the powers that be to bring my TARDIS down here ... It's not far away, at UNIT H.Q.'

'Just you leave it to me.' Winser marched towards the iron staircase with the air of a man determined to stand no nonsense.

The Doctor smiled, and looked at the casket of Axonite. 'And now for you, my friend,' he murmured quietly. The Doctor was sure Chinn wouldn't agree immediately—which meant Winser would be tied up for quite some time.

Carefully picking up the golden casket, the Doctor moved towards the Particle Accelerator.

He put the Axonite down on the console, and began adjusting control-settings. He had just pulled back the transparent door when he heard the lab door open. Presumably Winser had returned unexpectedly ... But when he looked up he saw that it wasn't Winser. It was Filer. 'Filer, my dear chap. Did you escape?' There was no reply. The Doctor looked again. The newcomer certainly *looked* like Filer, exactly like him. But he held himself with a certain stiffness, and the face was completely expressionless. The Doctor had encountered human replication before, during his battle with the Autons. So despite the amazing resemblance, he wasn't deceived by the creature that stalked towards him. This Filer was a fake.

The Doctor was even more sure when the replica spoke. The flatness of the voice was another give-away. 'Come with me, Doctor. You must come to Axos.'

'Nonsense,' said the Doctor briskly. 'I've no inten-

72

tion of coming with you anywhere. You're not Filer.'

'Come to Axos.' The replica seized the Doctor's arm in an iron grip, repeating the phrase like a broken record. 'You must come to Axos.'

The Doctor felt himself being dragged towards the laboratory door. Only his knowledge of Venusian Aikido enabled him to break free. He gripped the replica's arm, twisted, threw ... The fake Filer reeled across the laboratory and slammed into a bench, sending retorts and test tubes crashing to the floor.

A human being would have been stunned by such a fall. But the Axon stumbled to its feet and headed back towards the Doctor. 'You will come to Axos.' Its arm flashed out with amazing speed, clubbing the Doctor to the ground. The Axon began dragging him to the door.

Suddenly another, identical figure appeared in the doorway—the real Filer. The replica dropped the Doctor, and moved in to the attack.

Confronted by his double, Bill Filer reacted with swift efficiency. He sprang forward and delivered two swift chopping blows which should have knocked the creature out. It ignored the blows, moving forward remorselessly. Bill Filer backed away drawing his Colt Cobra. 'Doc, keep down,' he yelled, and pulled the trigger again and again.

The crash of the heavy revolver filled the laboratory. The impact of the bullets sent the replica staggering back—but that was all. Recovering its balance it stalked forward once more ...

Abandoning his gun, Filer closed with it. They fought fiercely, exchanging savage blows. Like the

73

Doctor before him, Filer found himself no match for the Axon's inhuman strength. He managed to trip it and send it staggering ... Filer grabbed a lab stool to smash down on the Axon—and the Doctor staggered dazedly to his feet and grabbed *him*. Desperately the real Filer yelled, 'No, Doc, no ... it's me!'

The Doctor realised he was wrestling with the real flesh and blood. Releasing Filer he swung round. They were just in front of the Particle Accelerator— and the Axon replica, on its feet once more, was rushing towards them. They jumped aside, Filer thrust out a foot—and the Axon shot straight through the open door of the Particle Accelerator. Quickly the Doctor slammed the door shut behind it, leaped to the power-lever and yanked it up to maximum.

Through the transparent door Filer looked on in horror at what seemed like his own destruction. The Axon replica disintegrated in the fierce blast of energy, turning first to a seething blob of Axonite, and then to a fine powdery dust. Shuddering, Filer turned away. 'I'm sure glad that wasn't me in there!'

The Doctor was at the control, closing down the Particle Accelerator. 'You're sure it isn't?'

'Am I *sure*? Doc, you don't think ...'

The Doctor grinned. 'No, I don't. Not as long as you go on calling me Doc. No Axon would ever be so frivolous!'

Somewhat belatedly an armed guard ran into the laboratory. The Doctor looked severely at him. 'I'm afraid you're too late, my man. The excitement's over. Now then, be so good as to take me to the Brigadier!'

*

The Master stood on a pedestrian footbridge which spanned the access road to Nuton Complex, studying the scene before him. His vantage point gave a good view of the main gate. Agitated sentries were running about like disturbed ants, and a stretcher-party was carrying away an unconscious body.

The Master had just seen the Axon replica of Filer gain entry to the Complex by clubbing down the sentry. Minutes later, he had seen the *real* Filer run through the unguarded gate. The Master smiled. It seemed almost certain that the clumsy Axon scheme to kidnap the Doctor had failed. Unfortunately it had stirred up the Nuton Complex so much that it was impossible for the Master to get in and deal with the Doctor himself.

He stood silently for a moment, pondering his next move, his black-clad figure almost invisible in the shadows. An army lorry drove slowly across the compound. The driver showed a pass to the sentries and drove out of the main gate, towards the bridge. Acting on impulse the Master climbed nimbly onto the railing of the footbridge. As the lorry passed beneath him he dropped neatly onto the roof.

The UNIT lorry rumbled steadily along the country roads. Glancing into his driving mirror, the driver suddenly saw not the road behind him but a face. A bearded face with dark burning eyes that stared into his own. A voice said, 'I am the Master. You will obey me. Pull into the side of the road.' For some reason it was impossible to disobey that voice. The driver did as he was told. Once the lorry was still, a black-clad figure climbed from the roof and into the passenger seat. A few minutes later, the lorry drove on its way.

As the ranking member of UNIT, the Brigadier had been confined in one of the Nuton Complex's VIP guest suites. Yates and Benton shared simpler quarters with the men. The Brigadier's accommodation was comfortable, even luxurious, but that didn't make imprisonment any less irksome. Watched by Jo, the Brigadier was pacing angrily to and fro, when he heard a familiar voice in the corridor outside. 'Good heavens, man, I know the Brigadier's incommunicado. I'm incommunicado myself. There's no reason why we can't talk to each other.'

In the corridor outside, the sentry was at a loss. Certainly there seemed no reason why one prisoner shouldn't talk to another prisoner ... To his relief, Captain Harker came along the corridor. 'All right, what's going on?' The Doctor repeated his demand to see the Brigadier. Harker considered. 'All right. Let him through.' The sentry opened the door and the Doctor went in. Filer was about to follow when Harker said politely. 'I'm sorry, sir, I don't think I know you.'

Hurriedly Filer produced an impressive-looking pass. 'Bill Filer, American Intelligence. I've got orders to interrogate these guys.'

Harker looked narrowly at him then nodded. 'Very well.' Filer followed the Doctor into the room, and the sentry closed the door. Harker lowered his voice. 'I'm by no means satisfied about all this. I'm going to

76

check with Mr Chinn. Keep them both here till I get back.'

Inside the suite the Doctor and his friends were having a rapid reunion. The Doctor was hurriedly bringing the Brigadier up to date with everything that had been happening. 'So you see,' the Doctor concluded, 'after Filer saw the Master inside Axos, the Axons copied *him*, and sent the replica to kidnap *me*. Then Filer, the real Filer, managed to escape— and he saw the Axons turning the Master loose.'

The Brigadier felt his head spinning with the flood of explanations. 'So what does all this mean, Doctor?'

'Well, for a start it means that the Axons' whole story is a pack of lies.'

'According to the Master they're some kind of space scavenger,' confirmed Filer. 'He said they'd destroy all life on Earth.'

'Which also means,' the Doctor continued, 'that we *must* keep Axonite confined to this Complex till we discover more about it.'

The door opened and Captain Harker came in. There was a revolver in his hand and an armed sentry behind him. 'Nobody move, please. Sentry, take this man's gun.' Filer handed over his revolver. Harker looked grimly at them. 'Well, you wanted to be here—and here you stay. My instructions are to confine you *all* in this suite.'

He was about to leave when the Doctor snapped, 'If you must "confine" me it had better be in the laboratory. I'm here to help with the Axonite experiments. Ask Doctor Winser if you don't believe me.'

'Doctor Winser happens to be in conference with Mr Chinn and Sir George Hardiman.'

'Then take me back to the laboratory, and check with Winser when he's free. Dammit man, you might at least put me back where you found me!'

Harker sighed. 'Very well, Doctor. You'll be confined to the laboratory. But no more expeditions please!'

The Doctor was hustled out. Jo and the Brigadier found themselves imprisoned once more—though this time with Filer for company. Jo squeezed his hand. 'Never mind, Bill. At least it's better than Axos.'

The Master watched a sweating squad of UNIT soldiers manhandle the Doctor's TARDIS onto a trolley and out of the laboratory. He smiled ironically to himself. The last time he had been in UNIT H.Q. it was in the disguise of a humble telephone engineer, on one of his unsuccessful attempts to kill the Doctor. It pleased him to return in a more exalted role—a visiting scientist from the Nuton Complex, vouched for by the UNIT lorry-driver.

A little simple hypnosis had soon extracted the driver's orders and ensured his further co-operation. The Master was scarcely able to believe his own luck. The lorry was on its way to UNIT to collect the TARDIS and take it back to the Nuton Complex. The Master had decided to allow the driver to carry out his mission—adding one or two little flourishes of his own.

He followed the trolley down the corridor then

turned off into another room where a puzzled UNIT R/T operator sat over his radio. For some time he had been trying to reach the Brigadier at his mobile H.Q. at Nuton. However he had only succeeded in reaching a stolid regular army operator who continually repeated that the Brigadier was 'not available.'

The operator looked up as the Master came into the room. 'Can I help you, sir?'

The Master smiled. 'You can indeed. I have an important message—for immediate world-wide distribution.'

'I'm sorry, sir. Only authorised personnel can use the international hook-up.'

The Master laid a hand on the operator's shoulder. 'Ah, but I'm a special case. I am the Master.' His voice hardened. 'I am the Master, and you will obey me ...'

A short time later, the UNIT lorry was speeding back towards Nuton, the tarpaulin-covered TARDIS in the back. The Master sat beside the driver, a satisfied smile playing on his lips. He found it very appropriate that the message which would mean the final doom of Earth had been sent from the heart of the organisation dedicated to its protection. One bird had been killed. It only remained to kill the other. When the TARDIS arrived at Nuton, the Doctor wouldn't be very far away. The Master smiled, and fingered the laser-gun beneath his coat.

7

The Axons Attack

Alone in Winser's laboratory, the Doctor was busy at the controls of the Particle Accelerator. The episode of the fake Filer had taken up valuable time. He wasn't sure how much longer he'd have the run of Winser's laboratory. As he worked, he delivered a running commentary into the control console's built-in tape recorder. 'My dear Winser,' he began, 'I do hope you will forgive this unauthorised use of your precious equipment. In case of anything going wrong, I have left you this recording of what *not* to do! I am now about to place the Axonite in the Accelerator ...'

The Doctor took the lid from the golden casket, opened the doors of the Particle Accelerator, and placed the container inside. Slamming the transparent doors, he continued recording. 'I am planning to split off a stream of Axonite particles and accelerate them through Time. I'm already linked to the computer, and my intention is to force the Axonite to analyse itself on the print-out.'

The Doctor closed his hand over the main power lever and began pulling it very slowly towards him. In dealing with the fake Filer he had been forced to subject the Axon creature to a single colossal blast of energy, simply in order to destroy it. The idea now was to *stimulate* the Axonite with a series of carefully *graduated* rises in particle acceleration. The Doctor wasn't quite sure what would happen— but he was pretty certain that *something* would . . .

His voice calm and steady, the Doctor continued recording, as he drew the power-lever slowly back. 'Reactor One activated. Accelerating . . . point one . . . two . . . three . . .' Inside the casket, the Axonite began to bubble and boil, sending off dazzling rays of multi- coloured light, like a burning jewel. A note of ex- citement came into the Doctor's voice. 'The Axonite is beginning to react . . .' He pulled the lever further towards him. 'Acceleration to speed of light . . . now!' Seething and bubbling the brightly-glowing Axonite overflowed the casket. In the laboratory, red lights flashed warningly, and the overload alarms began to ring . . .

In the nearby Axon ship the results of the Doctor's little experiment were even more dramatic. The Axon leader's golden face disintegrated into a streaming mass, as the stresses became too great for him to retain his personalised form. He stumbled towards the Brain. Around him the whole ship seemed to seethe and bubble, much like the Axonite in the Particle Accelerator. Since Axos and Axonite were one, the whole of Axos was disrupted. A shrill note of alarm filled the air.

As the Axon leader ran into the Brain area the Eye of Axos was lashing wildly to and fro on its stalk. There was hysteria in the whispering voice. 'Emer- gency, emergency! Nutrition cycle has been acti- vated prematurely. Immediate recovery of the Axonite sample is *essential, essential, essential* ...' The voice rose to a scream that echoed round the ship ...

His golden form now disintegrated into a many-tentacled mass, the Axon leader ran from the area.

In the Nuton Complex, alarm bells were ringing loudly. Captain Harker's first thought was that his prisoners must have escaped. He ran along to the guest suite, relieved to find the sentry still outside the door. 'Are the prisoners in there?'

'Far as I know, sir ... unless they've broken out by a window ...'

'We'd better check.'

The sentry opened the door, and Captain Harker ran inside—straight into an uppercut from the Brigadier that dropped him to the carpet, out cold. The astonished Filer acted by reflex, chopping down the sentry as he followed Harker into the room. Filer turned to the Brigadier, who was rubbing his knuckles. 'Hey, what's going on? Are we pulling a break-out?'

'Sudden impulse,' explained the Brigadier crisply. All at once I got very tired of being locked up. Now I must get a message through to the U.N. You two go and find the Doctor. I'll join you later.'

Stepping over the two prone bodies, the Brigadier marched briskly out of the room. Filer shrugged. 'Well, I guess we'd better do as he says. Where *is* the Doc?'

'I suppose he's still in the laboratory,' answered Jo. 'Let's go and see, shall we?'

Despite the clanging alarm bells, no one tried to

stop them as they ran to the laboratory. They found the Doctor in front of the throbbing Particle Accelerator, staring in total absorption at a pulsating blob of Axonite which had already grown enormously in size. Jo grabbed his arm, raising her voice above the whine of the machinery. 'What's going on, Doctor?'

He didn't seem in the least surprised to see her. 'Just a little test, Jo. Look at the Axonite! It's now taking the entire output of Reactor One and absorbing it. Absorbing the whole lot, and using it to grow ... Marvellous!'

There was a clatter of footsteps as Winser ran down the steps from the main control room. He didn't seem to share the Doctor's enthusiasm. In fact he was almost hysterical with rage. 'What's going on here?' With the strength of anger he flung the Doctor away from the controls. 'Get away from my equipment, you idiot. You're wrecking the whole apparatus!'

Slamming the power-lever back to close-down he ran to the transparent doors.

'Winser, *don't*,' yelled the Doctor. 'That's *live* Axonite in there!' He was too late. Winser flung open the doors—and the ever-growing blob of Axonite sucked him in and engulfed him. He vanished at once, totally absorbed by its seething mass.

Jo screamed and turned away in horror. The Doctor leaped to the transparent doors, and slammed them shut. Fascinated, he stood staring at the huge mass of Axonite swelling before them—still growing, despite the shut-down in power.

The Doctor spoke softly, almost to himself. 'It's just as I feared. The Axons, their ship, this Axonite ... They're all the same thing!'

Filer looked at him in disbelief. 'I don't get it, Doc.'

'We're dealing with a single living creature. The copy of you, Filer, the Axon you saw forming, Jo, *this* Axonite here—all part of the same organism. Axonite is just the dormant state.' The Doctor looked again at the still-growing mass. '*Was* the dormant state—until I activated it!'

The seething mass of Axonite began slamming itself against the doors. Filer whispered, 'Can't you stop it, Doc?'

'I've got to—or it could consume the whole planet. I only hope it's not too late ...'

With a shattering crash, the huge blob of Axonite burst open the heavy plastic doors and rolled slowly towards them like a giant boulder. They backed rapidly away. Jo looked behind them and screamed. Filling the laboratory door was the writhing, many-tentacled form of an Axon monster.

Filer acted by sheer instinct. With lunatic courage he shoulder-charged the monster, yelling, 'Doc, run. Get Jo out of here!'

Filer's sacrifice was in vain. One of the monster's tentacles slashed across his body, there was a fierce crackle of energy and Filer was hurled clear across the lab. Jo and the Doctor backed away as the monster bore down on them. The last thing they heard was the Voice of Axos. 'De-energise them!' Immediately the monster's tentacles lashed out and they were stunned into unconsciousness. The tentacles of the monster dragged them both away.

In Hardiman's empty office the Brigadier was on the

telephone. In a stunned voice he was saying, 'And you're absolutely sure? I see. Yes, of course, I'll take over at once.' Slowly he put down the phone, his mind reeling under the impact of shattering news. Some time ago a message had gone out from UNIT H.Q., not only to the U.N. Security Council, but to every Government and every news agency in the world. The message told of the Axon landing in England, and of the supreme benefits of Axonite, which were being offered not only to Great Britain, but to the entire planet.

The sensation and scandal had been immense. Now the entire world was insisting on immediate supplies of Axonite, threatening instant attack if the demands were not met. Great Britain had no alternative but to give way. The Brigadier was ordered to take over responsibility for security, pending a full enquiry into the leak. Chinn was to supervise distribution— acting purely as an administrator.

The Brigadier looked up as the door opened. Captain Harker stood in the doorway, covering him with a revolver. The Brigadier snapped, 'You can put that away, Captain. You won't be needing it.'

Harker rubbed the bruise on his jaw. 'You're still under arrest, Brigadier.'

'I very much doubt it.' The Brigadier passed Harker the telephone. 'Here—you'd better check with your H.Q. Whole situation's changed. Do as I say, man.'

The Brigadier watched as Harker made the call. He smiled grimly as a look of sheer astonishment spread slowly over the Captain's face.

*

In Winser's laboratory, everything was under control —*Axon* control. The seething mass of Axonite had disappeared—so too had Jo and the Doctor. Chinn and Sir George Hardiman rushed into the laboratory —to find the golden form of the Axon leader standing beside the Particle Accelerator.

Hardiman stared in amazement. 'What's been going on here? Where's Winser—and the Doctor?'

Gravely the Axon said, 'Your scientists have been killed. The female also.'

'Killed? How?'

'Their bodies were destroyed by an immense blast of radiation.' His voice was cold and angry. 'Our instruments showed that attempts were being made to interfere with the very structure of Axonite. Such experiments are dangerous in the extreme. We came to help—but we were too late.'

Hardiman looked round. 'We? But there's only you ...'

'My crew have taken the unstable material back to Axos where it can be safely destroyed. The radiation has already been neutralised.'

Chinn's immediate instinct was to find someone else to take the blame. 'Sir George, did you authorise these experiments?'

'I authorised normal tests, yes. But Winser went his own way. Besides ... I gather he had some kind of row with the Doctor fellow. Some experiment Winser thought too dangerous ... Maybe the Doctor——'

The stern voice of the Axon leader cut across their discussion. 'The blame is for you to decide. Such a thing must *never* happen again. *Never*. Otherwise we shall cancel the agreement—whatever the cost to ourselves.'

Jo and the Doctor recovered in the Axon cell that Filer and the Master had once occupied before them. Jo stirred, and immediately felt the restraining grip of the tentacles. The Axons had learned the lesson of Filer's escape. Now the tentacles reacted immediately to the slightest movement. As Jo struggled, their grip closed even tighter. She called out in panic, 'Doctor, I can't move. What are these things?'

The Doctor stood relaxed within his bonds, on the other side of the cell. 'We're inside Axos, Jo. The tentacles are part of Axos too.'

'Why have they brought us here? What do they want?'

The Doctor sighed. 'I only wish I knew.'

The golden figure of an Axon suddenly appeared in the doorway. 'Come!' The tentacles around them loosened their grip.

The Doctor moved away from the wall. 'Come along, Jo. I think we're about to meet our host!' Gripping her hand reassuringly, he led her from the cell. They followed the silent Axon down the glowing corridors.

The Brigadier was listening suspiciously to the Axon's story. 'So—by the time you arrived here, there was no sign of the Doctor or Miss Grant?'

The Axon leader shook his head. 'No one was here —except this man.' The Brigadier crossed to the crumpled body in the corner.

'Filer! Maybe he'll be able to tell us what happened.'

The Axon leader said, 'The man is gravely ill. It would be better if we were to take him back to our ship for treatment.'

'You will do no such thing. He'll be cared for in the medical wing here. See to it, will you please, Captain?'

Harker relayed the Brigadier's orders, and two soldiers began to carry Filer away.

Chinn was furious. 'You forget, Brigadier—you are no longer in a position to give orders.'

Captain Harker coughed. 'I'm afraid the position has changed, sir. I've had orders to hand over to the Brigadier.'

'New orders? I've heard nothing of this ...?'

'Well you have now,' barked the Brigadier. 'There's a lot of work in front of you, Mr Chinn. I suggest you contact your Minister.' As Chinn almost ran from the room, the Brigadier turned to Harker. 'Release Captain Yates and the rest of my men immediately. They will assist your own troops in making a search for the Doctor and Miss Grant.' He looked at the Axon leader. 'Despite this ... gentleman's theory, I am not yet convinced that they're dead.'

Jo cowered away from the terrifying scrutiny of the Eye of Axos. The Doctor however was quite calm, listening to the Voice with an expression of polite interest—rather like a guest whose host insists on telling him some rather lengthy anecdote.

'All things must die, Doctor,' whispered the Voice. 'Mankind ... this insignificant planet. Axos merely hastens the process a little.'

The Doctor raised an eyebrow. 'I see. May I ask how?' The Doctor had a pretty good idea of the answer to his question. But he was simply playing for time, seeking some way of escape. Despite his perilous position, it wasn't in his nature to give up.

The Voice of Axos continued its whispered explanation. 'Axonite is merely the bait for human greed. Because of that greed, Axonite will soon be spread across this entire planet. Then the nutrition cycle will begin.'

'And what happens then?'

'We shall consume every last particle of energy, every cell of living matter. Earth will be sucked dry.'

'I see,' said the Doctor coolly. 'So Axos is simply an overgrown cosmic parasite! Does this plan of yours have a time limit?'

'Axonite must be activated within seventy-two hours of our landing.'

The Doctor smiled at Jo. 'It looks as if our friend Chinn is doing the right thing—for the wrong reasons, of course.'

'What do you mean?' asked Jo shakily.

'For purely selfish reasons, he intends to confine the supply of Axonite to Great Britain.'

There was triumph in the whispering voice. 'No longer, Doctor. That too has been taken care of.'

'Indeed? Well, am I here purely as an audience for your boastings—or do you have something else in mind?'

'You are here because you have knowledge that we

need, Doctor. Knowledge of Time travel.'

Chinn listened shuddering to the Minister's angry voice. 'The whole thing has blown up in our faces, Chinn. There has been a catastrophic security leak. The world is insisting on immediate distribution of Axonite. It will take place immediately. *You* will see to it.'

'Yes, sir. As soon as ...'

'Never mind "as soon as", Chinn. Now!'

'You can depend on me, sir!'

'Well, just in case we can't—your resignation is on my desk, Chinn. I've written it out myself. All it needs is your signature!'

There was a click and the line went dead. Chinn slammed down the phone, and buried his head in his hands. Then he took a deep breath, rallying himself.

He snatched up the phone again. 'Get me Air Transport command. This is Chinn, here—from the Ministry.'

Sadly Sergeant Benton looked on, as a squad of soldiers carried the familiar blue shape of the TARDIS into the corner of Winser's laboratory. Much use it was now, with the Doctor nowhere to be found. 'All right, lads, that'll do.' He turned to the man beside him. His voice was very respectful, for the figure beside him, overcoat collar turned up and cap pulled low, wore the uniform of a General. 'I still think I ought to tell the Brigadier you're here, sir.'

A clipped military voice snapped, 'You will do no such thing, sergeant. That is a direct order. This is a surprise inspection. I shall contact the Brigadier myself when I see fit. Now, where's your Scientific Adviser, this Doctor fellow?'

General or no General, Benton wasn't going to tell his mysterious visitor more than necessary. 'I'm afraid I don't know, sir,' he said—which was true enough.

'Well, find him and send him in here to me. Meanwhile, see I'm not disturbed.'

The General turned away dismissively. Benton said, 'Very good, sir,' saluted and left the laboratory.

As soon as he was gone, the Master took off his cap and greatcoat and tossed them over a stool. He crossed to the TARDIS, took a complicated electronic device from his pocket and spent the next few minutes picking the lock. When at last it gave way, he went into the TARDIS, closing the door behind him.

Once inside, the Master paused, looking round the control room in horror. It was certainly in something of a mess, the control console partly dismantled, wires and electronic circuits scattered everywhere. The Master shook his head in disgust. 'Oh no! What *has* he been trying to do?' He knew the answer well enough. The Doctor had been trying to evade the Time Lords sentence of exile and get his TARDIS going again. 'What a botch up!' He kicked the console savagely. 'Of all the mouldering moth-eaten, clapped out piles of obsolete old junk! Still, perhaps, it *could* be made to work—just possibly. If there's no alternative.'

Sadly the Master thought of his own gleaming immaculate TARDIS, one of the latest models, still held fast in the grip of Axos. He drew the stubby laser-gun from his pocket, and stroked it gently. 'Now then, Doctor, where are you? Don't keep me waiting too long ...'

The Doctor was conducting a desperate mental duel with the Brain of Axos.

'I couldn't help you if I wanted to,' he protested. 'The Time Lords took away my knowledge of Time travel when they exiled me to this planet.'

'It is useless to lie, Doctor,' hissed the Voice. 'Not *all* of your knowledge was taken from you. Besides ...' The Voice took on a seductive note, 'We have explored the blocks on your memory. It is possible that we can free them. We must have the secret of Time travel. We *must*!'

'Must you? Why?'

'To expand our feeding range!' Greedily the Voice hissed, 'Soon it will be necessary to enlarge the energy sources available to us. Time travel will give us the power to range through all Time. Axos will be immortal, indestructible!'

The Doctor shuddered at the thought of this voracious monster roaming not only Space but Time to devour its prey. Defiantly he shouted, 'I refuse to ally myself to ... to such cosmic bacteria!'

'*We shall see.*' Tentacles lashed round Jo and the Doctor, holding them powerless. 'Are you aware, Doctor, that Axonite can absorb the very life-force of a human being? We have arranged a demonstration for you. You shall see your companion age to death.'

There was a crackle of energy and Jo went rigid,

her eyes staring before her. The Doctor struggled wildly, but he was firmly held. Helplessly he watched as wrinkles and cracks appeared in Jo's face. Her skin sagged, her hair went first grey, then white ... her body twisted into a crouch. It was like watching a speeded-up film of the effect of the passing years. Jo looked thirty, forty, fifty, sixty, seventy ... she was turning into a wizened old woman before his eyes. Soon she would be dead.

8

The Power Robbers

Eighty, ninety, one hundred ... Jo Grant was withering into old age. The Voice of Axos whispered, 'The process *can* be reversed, Doctor, but only if it is arrested in time ...'

The Doctor shouted. 'Stop! For pity's sake, let her alone.'

'You will co-operate?'

'I *can't* co-operate. Not even Axos can defy the Laws of Time. Give me a chance and I'll prove it to you.'

'Very well.'

Jo's body seemed to freeze. She began to straighten up. Her hair went from white to grey, then back to brown. Her skin smoothed out, cracks and wrinkles disappeared ... Suddenly she was young again. The Doctor sighed with relief. Jo stared round wildly, aware that something had been happening, but not sure what. 'Doctor? I felt so strange ...'

'Don't worry, Jo, it's over. You're all right now.'

Impatiently the Voice of Axos hissed, 'Begin, Doctor. *Begin!*'

'What do you want me to do?'

'Concentrate! You have only to *think* the Time Equations. The mind of Axos will do the rest.'

The Doctor wasn't surprised. He had already guessed that Axos had a degree of telepathic ability.

'I assume you know the basic theories? In fact, you already have the power of Time travel—to a very limited extent.'

'How did you know that?' There was surprise in the Voice.

The Doctor smiled. 'I knew from the moment you eluded the human missiles. How else could you have done that, but by a Time jump? You reached Earth *before* the missiles were fired.'

'That is so. But we can move only moments in Time. It is not enough. Begin!'

The Doctor stared deep into the Eye.

Jo looked on, only half-aware of what was happening. She saw an area behind the Eye turn into a kind of screen, across which flowed a stream of complicated equations.

The Voice said, 'Good. And the power requirements?' More equations. Now the Voice was angry. 'What is this, Doctor? Remember what will happen if you lie.'

'Pure mathematics cannot lie. You need a colossal amount of power to create a Time Field for a being as large as Axos. Look!' Another equation filled the screen. Even Jo's shaky grasp of mathematics was enough to tell her that it represented an immense quantity of power. 'There,' said the Doctor triumphantly. 'Your final power requirements—well in excess of your total capacity.'

There was a long pause, then the Voice said, 'All data confirmed.'

The Doctor waved towards the screen. 'There you are then. You might just as well abandon the idea of Time travel.'

The Voice spoke again. 'Add the total output of the Nuton Power Complex to your figures, Doctor.'

'If you wish. Though there's very little point.'

The equations changed again. The Voice said exultantly, 'Data confirms Time travel attainable using additional power from Complex. And we can call upon the whole of Nuton's power whenever we need it.'

'How? You can scarcely just walk in and take it.'

Gloatingly the Voice hissed, 'On the contrary, Doctor—we *can*!'

A huge map of the world had been installed on the wall of Hardiman's office. Hardiman was at a conference in London. Around his big office table sat Chinn, the Brigadier, and the golden figure of the Axon leader. The Brigadier was making a final, useless protest. 'In my view the whole question of Axonite's distribution should be shelved until we find the Doctor, and get his report on it' The Brigadier had recovered much of his confidence, and Chinn was his old objectionable self again.

'The Doctor! We shan't be seeing *that* gentleman again. If he wasn't killed in the explosion, then he's simply cleared off.'

'We have still to search the Axon ship——'

Smoothly the Axon intervened. 'At the present time, our energies are fully occupied with providing the Axonite your planet demands. Mr Chinn, perhaps you would show me the extent of your operation?'

Eagerly Chinn rose. 'Yes, of course. A very efficient set-up, if I do say so myself.' He took up a pointer and touched it to the map. 'Cape Kennedy, Ottowa, Baikonur, Lop Nor ...' The string of names droned on and on ... Chinn ended with a triumphant flourish of his pointer. 'There you are, gentlemen! Axonite consignments are now on their way to every major scientific establishment on this planet.'

A smile curled the golden lips of the Axon leader. He thought of all those units of Axonite suddenly coming alive when the Nutrition Cycle was triggered. Breaking out of their containers, feeding, growing. Sucking up every atom of energy, and returning with it to Axos. Then and only then would Axos depart, leaving behind it the dead husk of a planet. 'Excellent. Truly excellent.'

Chinn smiled complacently. 'Thank you,' he said, with unconvincing modesty. 'Just doing my job.'

Suddenly the Axon leader went still. In his head there was a commanding Voice. 'Depersonalise. Locate and enter main reactor. Establish link and transmit power.' The Axon strode abruptly from the room.

Chinn, who was still looking at the map, turned and said, 'Yes, I think that more or less wraps it ...' He broke off, realising that the Axon was no longer there. 'Funny chap, that ...'

The Brigadier snorted. 'I'm off to see Filer in the medical wing. I gather they're expecting him to come round about now.'

The Brigadier marched from the room. Chinn was left alone with his map. He was quite unaware that his efforts had brought considerably nearer the total destruction of Earth.

Filer had indeed recovered. Still pale and shaky,

watched over by a hovering nurse, he gave the Brigadier the true story of the events in Winser's laboratory.

The Brigadier was highly delighted. 'So the Doctor and Miss Grant *weren't* killed?'

'They sure weren't. The Axonite got Winser—then that spaghetti-monster turned up and clobbered me. My guess is the Axons have got them.'

'The Doctor definitely said Axonite was dangerous?'

'Sure! Said it could drain all the energy from the planet.'

The Brigadier stood up. 'I'm off for a word with Chinn—not to mention our Axon *friends*. Maybe we can still stop distribution. Stay here and rest, Filer.'

'Not on your life,' yelled Filer. But the Brigadier was gone. Filer turned on the hovering nurse. 'Don't just stand there, Florence Nightingale. Get me my clothes!'

The Axon leader moved between the concrete buildings of the Nuton Complex. His humanoid form was already dissolving into a monstrous many-tentacled figure, the Axons' basic shape.

The golden appearance was assumed only to reassure humans, and maintaining that shape took up much of the Axon's strength. He needed all his energy for the task before him.

A UNIT guard appeared, and stopped at the sight of the horror lurching towards him. He raised his rifle but the monster was already upon him. A lashing tentacle, a surge of energy and the guard crumpled to the ground. The Axon moved on.

Nuton's Main Reactor was housed in a squat, blank-walled building with massive steel doors. Two bored sentries were on patrol. Boredom changed to unbelieving terror as the Axon monster turned the corner of the building and came rushing towards them.

Shaking off their fear, they opened fire. They poured shot after shot into the heaving tentacled mass, with absolutely no effect. The monster seemed to *flow* towards them ... One of the sentries fled in panic. The other hesitated too long and was blasted to extinction by the Axon monster's tentacle.

The creature moved up to the massive steel doors. Its tentacles flailed out, there was a massive surge of energy, and the doors sprang open.

Returning from the medical wing, the Brigadier heard the rattle of gunfire. Drawing his revolver he set off at a run. He ran straight into the fleeing sentry, and grabbed him by the shoulders. 'Pull yourself together, man. What happened?'

The sentry pointed a shaking hand behind him. 'Killed my mate, sir. It just went in there ... *inside the Reactor*!'

The Brigadier let the man go and sprinted for the Reactor. He saw the steel doors hanging open and peered cautiously inside. At the end of a concrete-lined corridor the Axon monster crouched by a heavy, lead-shielded door. The Brigadier was just in time to see the door fly open, there was a glare of light ... and the Axon disappeared. Shaking his head in disbelief,

the Brigadier turned and ran back to the adminis-
tration buildings.

As he arrived outside the main block, a car drew
up and Sir George Hardiman stepped out. The
Brigadier ran up to him. 'Sir George, come with
me!'

'What's happened? What's going on?'

'I want you to check the Main Reactor.'

'Then we'll have to go to the control room. What
is going on, Brigadier?'

The Brigadier bustled the astonished Hardiman
over to the laboratory block and into the control
room. 'I'm sorry, sir, this really is urgent.'

'Oh, very well!' Watched by a puzzled technician
Hardiman began checking the maze of dials and
meters that lined the walls of the reactor control
room. Suddenly he broke off, peering through the
picture window. 'I say, why is there a police box in
Winser's laboratory?'

'Part of the Doctor's equipment. The Reactor, Sir
George!'

Hardiman completed his check. 'Everything seems
pretty much in order. The readings are *slightly* up
... Now, what *is* this all about?'

'Our Axon friend has just walked straight into the
furnace of the Main Reactor.'

Hardiman looked at the Brigadier as if he was mad.

Inside the TARDIS, the Master straightened up with
a groan. 'Hopeless! Over-weight ... underpowered
... museum piece!' He pulled a lever and the
TARDIS console vibrated alarmingly. Hurriedly the

Master switched it off. 'Might as well try to fly a second-hand gas stove!'

He turned on the scanner. Rather to his surprise it actually worked. The Master scanned round the laboratory, zooming in on a close-up of the Particle Accelerator. 'Now that *is* interesting. If I cannibalise some of the parts ...'

The Master had never had the slightest hesitation in helping himself to other people's property. He collected tools from the Doctor's locker and opened the TARDIS door.

Hardiman said obstinately, 'If the Axon *did* go into the Main Reactor, then he's simply committed suicide. No living being could survive the energies ...'

Captain Yates had come into the control room. Suddenly he called. 'Look, sir! In the laboratory.' A black-clad figure was calmly dismantling the Particle Accelerator. 'It's the Master, sir!'

The Brigadier drew his revolver. 'So it is. And this time—we've got him!'

9

The Sacrifice

Absorbed in trying to dismantle the laser-trigger
from the light accelerator, the Master was unaware of
the Brigadier and Yates creeping down the iron staircase and across the laboratory towards him.

Hardiman appeared at the top of the staircase, yelling, 'Brigadier! There's a massive power surge in
the Main Reactor!'

Alerted, the Master spun round, only to find the
Brigadier covering him with his revolver. He made a
dive for the TARDIS, but Yates blocked his way.
The Master snatched out his laser gun. 'Drop that
thing or I'll blow your head off!' The Brigadier
levelled his revolver.

The Master considered the odds then shrugged.
As always, he preferred to live and fight another day.
He tossed the laser gun to the floor and the Brigadier
picked it up. 'Now then—what are you doing here?
What are you after?'

The Master nodded towards the TARDIS. 'That—
unfortunately.'

'You wanted to steal the TARDIS?'

The Master shrugged. 'My own is in the hands of
Axos. I needed a vehicle with which to leave this
planet—before it's too late.'

'But why bring it here?'

'That was the Doctor's idea. By the way, I'd hoped

for the pleasure of meeting him ... just once more. Where is he?'

'In the hands of the Axons, like your TARDIS.'

Hardiman came running down the ladder, near-panic in his voice. 'Brigadier, don't you realise? There's an uncontrollable power build-up in the Main Reactor, it could go critical at any moment. The whole place will blow up.'

'What's happened?' Such was the authority in the Master's voice that the Brigadier told him. The Master nodded. 'I'm afraid the Axons have taken over your Reactor. They're stealing its energy for some purpose of their own.'

Hardiman was on the verge of panic. 'They don't understand the dangers involved. They'll kill us all if it overloads.'

The Brigadier looked at the Master. 'You! You know these creatures. Is there anything we can do to stop them? It's your life too, remember.'

'I'm afraid there's nothing *you* can do. There might be something I can do ... in exchange for my freedom.' The Master glanced meaningly at the Brigadier's revolver.

'That's quite impossible.'

The Master sighed regretfully. 'Then in that case ...' He leaned back against the wall, folding his arms. 'We'll all go up together!'

Urgently Hardiman whispered, 'Brigadier, if this place goes up it will cost untold numbers of lives. All it needs is a chain reaction and this whole complex will become an enormous nuclear bomb.'

The Master gave a judicious nod. 'I'm afraid he's right, Brigadier.'

Hardiman grabbed the Brigadier's arm. 'For heaven's sake—if there's a chance this man can help give him whatever he wants.'

The Brigadier looked agonised at the thought of losing his prisoner so soon. But there was really no choice. 'Very well.'

'My absolute and unconditional freedom?' insisted the Master.

'*Yes!* Now get moving!' Reluctantly the Brigadier holstered his revolver.

The Master turned to Hardiman. 'Listen carefully. I want a power-link from the Main Reactor into the TARDIS.'

Hardiman was boggled. 'How will that help?'

'I shall store up the power, then boost it through the Accelerator and back to Axos. Instead of a gradual build-up the Axons will get it all in one devastating surge.'

'Is there anything else we can do?'

'Oh, you might try the usual nuclear blast precautions—sticky tape on the windows, that sort of thing . . .'

The Master opened the TARDIS door, just as Filer ran into the lab. Bill Filer's arms instructor would have been proud of him. When he saw the Master, he made the fastest draw of his life. As if by magic, the Colt Cobra was in Filer's hand and jammed behind the Master's ear. 'O.K., brother, hold it right there.'

The Master sighed wearily. 'Really, Brigadier, do you want my help or don't you? I really can't concentrate with these constant interruptions.'

Regretfully the Brigadier said, 'Put the gun away, Filer.'

'But this guy's the *Master*. Don't you realise——'

'I know. For the moment we happen to need his help.'

'*He's* helping you? Are you crazy, Brigadier?'

'Very probably, Mr Filer. But we don't seem to have any choice.'

'But ...' Filer couldn't believe that his prey was going to slip through his fingers yet again.

'No buts,' said the Brigadier firmly. 'Put the gun away, Mr Filer.'

Numbly Filer obeyed.

'Thank you,' said the Master acidly. 'Now perhaps I can get to work.'

Once again, he started to enter the TARDIS.

Hardiman was making for the control room. 'I'll set up the link at once.' He paused, looking back at the Master. 'Where will you be?'

The Master opened the TARDIS door. 'In here.'

Hardiman was baffled. 'In there? Why?'

'Because theoretically this contraption should be able to store the energy generated around it. Think of it as a giant battery!'

For the first time Hardiman seemed to take in the Master's plan. 'Are you trying to tell me you can store the entire output of my Main Reactor in a—police box?'

'Oh yes,' said the Master gently. 'At least, I hope so. It'll be just too bad for all of us if I'm wrong.'

He disappeared inside the TARDIS and closed the door.

*

In the Brain area of Axos there was frantic activity. The whole of Axos hummed with energy. The Doctor looked on in an agony of remorse. He had given the Axons the Time travel equations in the certainty that they would never be able to use them. But he'd underestimated them. Somehow they *were* getting the power they needed.

He watched intently as the power-equations flashed across the screen. The Voice of Axos whispered, 'Forty per cent Time Field capability. Forty-five per cent ...' Then, 'Sixty per cent ... Fifty per cent ...' The Voice changed. 'Emergency, emergency!'

The Doctor looked hopefully at Jo. 'Something's going wrong. They're not getting the power through!'

The Voice of Axos began issuing a rapid stream of orders. 'Locate power failure source. Investigate possible cell damage. Evaluate, trace and restore all energy absorption channels. Emergency, Emergency ...'

Suddenly the Doctor realised that the tendrils holding him were beginning to slacken their grip. So totally was Axos involved in the crisis that even the tiny amount of power needed to hold its prisoners was leaking away. Slowly he edged free, gesturing to Jo to do the same. Once they were clear of the tendrils he grabbed Jo's hand and they set off at a run.

Luckily for them, the Brain of Axos could spare them only a little of its attention. 'Attention, Time Lord and companion escaping. Close all exit tracts. Surround, neutralise and retrieve once emergency is over!'

The Doctor and Jo fled through the glowing corridors, somehow managing to elude the tendrils that lashed out to catch them. Axos was confused and distracted. While that distraction lasted, there was a chance, just a chance, that they might win free.

A powerful throb of energy was shaking the laboratory. Massive cables ran from the Reactor into the TARDIS. Hardiman stood by the control console, monitoring the enormous flow of power. Somehow the Master's extraordinary set-up was working. The Main Reactor's output was flowing *not* to Axos but into the TARDIS. Helplessly the Brigadier looked on. Hardiman looked up at him, raising his voice above the deep throbbing hum. 'It can't take much more, Brigadier. It *can't!*'

Inside the TARDIS, the Master presided over the rocking, throbbing TARDIS control-console like the captain of a ship in a typhoon. He could see the Brigadier and Hardiman on the scanner. Hardiman was saying, 'I daren't feed in much more. I don't want to risk the cables burning out!'

The Master switched on the TARDIS loudspeaker system and yelled, 'Risk the cables, man! Risk everything! We've got to!' As his fingers flashed over the TARDIS console, the Master was actually smiling. He liked a good crisis. In his own peculiar way, he was enjoying himself.

Jo and the Doctor found their progress slower. More and more tendrils reached out for them, and the walls seemed to be closing in. Suddenly the narrow space through which they were squeezing turned into a dead end. Tentacles wound round them, holding them trapped. They were prisoners once more.

The Master was outside the TARDIS now, working on the connections to the Particle Accelerator. He finished making adjustments to the main power lever and looked at his worried audience—Yates, Hardiman and the Brigadier. 'I've adapted the power lever so that it will free the vast surge of energy now stored inside the TARDIS. When that energy is released it will surge back to Axos in one enormous boost!'

Hardiman asked, 'And what will that do to Axos?'

'Cripple it, I hope. Perhaps even kill it. Let's see, shall we?'

The Master's hand stretched out for the power-lever. Suddenly the Brigadier knocked it away. 'Just one moment. We have reason to believe that the Doctor and Miss Grant are prisoners inside Axos. What will happen to them?'

The Master smiled. 'I was wondering when that would occur to you, Brigadier. There is one slight disadvantage to my plan. When the power-surge hits Axos, the Doctor and Miss Grant will die. They won't stand a chance.'

In a horrified voice the Brigadier said, 'No, I won't let you do it.'

The Master sounded calm, almost amused. Clearly he was enjoying the situation. 'The choice *is* yours—but remember ... unless we deal with this crisis, the whole complex will explode. And that's just part of it. Unless we destroy Axos, Brigadier—Axos will destroy the world!'

The Brigadier stood very still. Once again, there *was* no choice. How could he set the lives of two people against the life of the world? He stepped away from the console.

The Master reached out and pulled the lever.

10

Brainstorm

Axos convulsed.

The massive, unexpected surge of energy *almost* crippled it, *almost* killed it. But not quite. Summoning all its resources Axos began to fight back ...

In the middle of the energy storm that lashed through Axos, Jo and the Doctor found themselves free again. The Doctor grabbed Jo's hand and dragged her through the chaos. All around them Axos seethed and pulsed. Even the surface beneath them *rolled* in waves of movement. A kaleidoscope of flashing lights spun before them, and a mad, high-pitched screaming filled their ears. Jo sobbed, 'Doctor, I can't take any more.'

Ruthlessly the Doctor urged her on. 'Keep going, Jo, we'll die if we stop.'

Jo collapsed, her hands over her face. She began sobbing hysterically. The Doctor heaved her to her feet and shook her roughly. 'Stop it, Jo. We *must* keep going.'

She shook her head to clear it. 'What's that screaming noise?'

'Axos,' said the Doctor simply. 'The whole creature's electro-convulsing. The power's creating an electric storm in the brain. We're going straight through the centre of the trauma. Look here!'

Their flight had taken them back into the Brain

area, the heart of the power-storm. The agonising pain of Axos showed itself as patterns of liquid light, flowing across the walls. The Eye lashed to and fro on its stalk, totally uncontrolled. Jo felt the pain and the near-madness of Axos reaching into her mind, overwhelming her ... She staggered, clutching her head.

'Fight it, Jo,' shouted the Doctor. 'Don't let it get a grip on your mind. Listen to me ... Three sevens ... What's three sevens? *Tell me!*'

All the time he was pulling her onwards.

Jo found that concentration on the absurdly simple sum *did* help to withstand the barrage of sound and light stimuli all around her. 'Twenty-one ...' she muttered. 'Three sevens are *twenty-one* ...'

They fought their way across the Brain area and into an outer chamber. Here too everything was a chaotic turmoil of light and sound. Jo reeled back ...

'Times *four*,' called the Doctor. 'Now multiply by *four*.'

Jo grappled with the problem, her eyes tight shut against those terrible anguished patterns of light. It was harder this time '... Eighty ... *eighty-four*' she gasped triumphantly.

'Well done—now—divide by six!'

So they struggled on, the Doctor firing off sums, Jo forcing herself to answer them. At last they reached an opening on the far side of the chamber. The Doctor helped Jo through it, and they started down the long tunnel beyond.

He paused as they came to a fork. 'I think there's a way out down here ...'

They ran along the tunnel, which seemed to sway

to and fro as they moved along. A shapeless figure appeared, lurching towards them. Jo cowered back against the wall. It was an Axon, part golden humanoid, part tentacled monster. It reeled almost blindly ahead, lashing feebly at them. The Doctor ducked, and gave it a hearty shove. The already decomposing Axon slammed into the wall, then slid to the floor, dissolving into a shapeless puddle of Axonite. Jo covered her eyes ...

The Doctor took her hand and led her past. 'Come on, Jo. We're nearly there now.'

They reached a wider passage. At the end of it they recognised the arched door that led to freedom. The door was steadily shrinking as though it was trying to close itself, but couldn't quite summon up the energy.

'Quick,' shouted the Doctor. 'It's closing up!'

Desperate to escape, Jo ran for the door and shot through the fast-shrinking opening in a flying leap. The Doctor was close behind her. As they hurtled through the gap, it closed convulsively behind them, in a last-minute attempt to prevent their escape. But too late. They were free! Picking themselves up they ran towards the Nuton Complex.

Meanwhile, Axos was fighting back. The sudden unexpected surge of power was slowly being absorbed, *controlled*. The panic began to subside, the Brain began functioning once more.

Weakly the Voice of Axos whispered. 'Source of attack identified. Power-surge is being channelled through Particle Accelerator. Concentrate power-reversal on this sector. Total destruction essential— repeat—*essential*!'

*

The Master stepped out of the TARDIS and looked round the silent laboratory. 'Well, gentlemen? Your congratulations would be in order, I think?'

The Brigadier, Captain Yates and Bill Filer looked grimly back at him. No one spoke.

'I see. How very ungracious. Well, if you'll forgive me I have a few minor repairs to complete.' The Master turned to re-enter the TARDIS.

The Brigadier stepped forward. 'Wait!'

'Why? You agreed to my freedom, and now I've earned it.'

'We don't know that yet. Until we're sure what's happened ...'

'Really, Brigadier, I promised to help you solve this crisis. I can't solve *all* your problems for you.'

The Brigadier was unmoved. 'Captain Yates!'

Yates's revolver was already covering the Master.

Hardiman appeared at the top of the steps. 'Something's going wrong, Brigadier. They've absorbed the power, and now they're feeding it back to us!' He ran to the control room and flicked the switch of a public-address system. 'This is Sir George Hardiman. All personnel, your attention, please. Evacuate Accelerator sector. Shut off all power and proceed to blast-wall shelters. That is all.'

He ran back to the laboratory. The Particle Accelerator started throbbing with power once more, and the cable-connections were beginning to smoke. The power-throb rose higher and higher ...

Hardiman took command. 'Into the main control room, everybody!'

The Brigadier watched him go to a locker and put

on protective goggles and heavy gloves. 'What are you going to do?

'Disconnect those cables. Now, the control room, please, Brigadier.'

The Brigadier looked at the rapidly-vibrating Particle Accelerator. The cables were pouring out smoke now and it was clearly dangerous even to touch them. 'Let me help you.'

'No, Brigadier, this is my responsibility. I'm a scientist or I used to be. I'll join you as soon as I've finished.'

'Very well.' The Brigadier waved to Yates and Filer, who herded the Master up the stairs at gunpoint. The Brigadier followed, turning at the top of the stairs. 'Good luck, Sir George.' Hardiman didn't hear him. Gloves and goggles looking incongruous with his immaculate suit, he was bending over the shuddering console, a pair of insulated pliers in his hands. The Brigadier ran to the control room and joined the others.

They watched through the picture window as Hardiman worked steadily at his task, seemingly unaffected by the din all round him. The power-hum had risen to a roar that was shaking the whole building. Tensely the Brigadier asked, 'How's he doing?'

'Surprisingly well,' answered the Master. 'He'll have to take the trigger section out before he can disconnect the main cable. It's a tricky job ...'

'How much time has he got?'

'Who knows, Brigadier? Who knows?'

Hardiman pushed up the goggles to wipe the sweat from his eyes, replaced them and went on with his task. It was a very long time since he'd last had tools in his hands, but he worked calmly and steadily, with a curious feeling of contentment. Despite all the years in meetings and conferences, he could still do a real job when he had to ... Like a man defusing a bomb, he unscrewed the last bolt and lifted the trigger-section free. Gently he lowered it to the floor.

The Brigadier shouted, 'He's done it!'

'Almost,' said the Master softly. 'Almost—but not quite. There's still the main power cable ...'

The cable was very hot now, and Hardiman's gloves were starting to smoulder. Carefully he unbolted the shackles and tugged. The cable refused to come free—the shackles had been warped by the heat. He tugged again ... and again. He gave a final heave. There was a sudden explosion that hurled him clear across the room—but the main power cable was free, the end clutched in his gloved hand. The roaring stopped, leaving a silence that hurt the ears.

The spectators in the control room rushed down into the laboratory. Yates ran across to Hardiman and knelt beside the body. 'He's dead, sir. The shock must have killed him instantly.'

The Brigadier nodded silently. Filer yelled, 'Look out!' The Master, who had been last to leave the control room, was running for the TARDIS.

Filer ran to tackle him, but the Master smashed him to one side. But by now Yates and the Brigadier were blocking the way to the TARDIS. The Master changed direction, and ran for the door. He almost made it—then an out-thrust foot brought him crashing down. He looked up. In the doorway stood a tall figure, grimy and rumpled, but still with a certain elegance. 'Dear me!' said the Doctor. 'Leaving so soon?'

The Brigadier commandeered Hardiman's office for a combined meal and conference. The Doctor, Yates, Filer, Jo Grant and, of course, Chinn, sat round a big conference table tucking into much needed coffee and sandwiches. The Master, handcuffed, was an unwilling spectator. Also present was Ericson, a balding unobtrusive man who'd been Hardiman's assistant, and was now considerably alarmed to find himself in full charge.

The Doctor, happily munching a chicken sandwich, offered one to the Master, who snarlingly refused. 'Temper!' said the Doctor reprovingly, and took a swig of coffee. 'Now then, Brigadier, you've sent out those warnings about Axonite?'

'I've sent them out—whether any one will believe them is another matter. There's a tendency to regard them as a trick to regain control of Axonite.'

The Doctor nodded. 'Very understandable, considering the earlier behaviour of friend Chinn.'

Chinn glowered into his coffee cup, but said nothing. So much had gone so drastically wrong, that he was laying very low till the situation cleared. If there was any credit going, he could always grab it later.

The Doctor put down his cup. 'Well, that aside, we've enough to worry about with the main body of Axos—here.' He gestured through the window in the direction of the mound. 'Axos is like a vulture, gentlemen,' said the Doctor dramatically. 'Its claws are already sunk deep into your planet and it has no intention of letting go. Soon it will activate the Nutrition Cycle—and the feast will begin!'

Whatever that meant, Filer didn't like the sound of it. 'How's that again, Doc?'

'The Axonite will cease to be dormant. It will begin to feed, and continue till every scrap of energy, every living thing has been consumed.'

Ever-practical, the Brigadier asked, 'Well? How do we stop it?' He seemed quite confident that the Doctor would have an answer.

'I'm not sure that we can.'

Jo was horrified. 'There must be *something* you can do, Doctor?'

'I can try.' He turned to Ericson. 'Can you commandeer the computer banks for me? I'll need to make some very complex calculations.'

Ericson nodded. 'Yes, of course, Doctor. I'll clear them right away.'

'Good, that's a start. Now then, Brigadier, I want you to keep constant watch on Axos. We must know its every move.'

The Brigadier looked across the table. 'Captain Yates, will you see to that?'

'Right away, sir. There's remote-control camera equipment in the Mobile H.Q. We could use that.'

'Off you go then. I'll be setting up my H.Q. in the lab. I want you in R/T contact all the time.'

The Doctor stood up. 'Then that's it for the moment. Oh, just one more thing—I'm afraid I'll need *him*.' He pointed to the Master.

Immediately Filer protested, 'Now just a minute, Doc . . .'.

'I'm sorry, Bill. You'll have to hand him over. The

only way I can defeat Axos is by using the TARDIS. To do that I must have the Master's help. He has certain knowledge that is no longer available to me.' The Doctor smiled. 'Anyway, he's quite a competent mechanic. He may as well earn his keep!'

The Master shot him a murderous glance, but said nothing. Reluctantly, Filer unlocked the Master's handcuffs. Jo leaned closer to the Doctor. 'How can you possibly trust him?' she whispered. 'You know he'll kill you first chance he gets.'

The Doctor gave her a reassuring pat on the head. 'Don't worry, Jo. The Brigadier's given me this.' He produced the Master's laser gun. 'That'll keep him in order.'

But Jo wasn't reassured. The Doctor was quite unused to carrying weapons, let alone using them. She couldn't help feeling that his nature was no match for the Master's evil cunning. Like Filer, she was very worried as she watched the Master follow the Doctor from the room.

Loaded down with camera equipment, Captain Yates and Sergeant Benton struggled to the top of a low wooded rise and peered over the edge. Benton said, 'Right on target.' There below them was the low mound which was all that could be seen of Axos. 'It doesn't seem to be doing anything, sir. Just sitting there.'

'Let's hope it goes on doing just that, Sergeant,' whispered Yates. 'Well, on with the show. Our viewers are waiting!' They set up the camera at a convenient vantage point, camouflaging it as best they could with rocks and branches. Then they moved carefully back down the ridge, laying cable behind them, until they reached their Land Rover which was hidden in a clump of bushes.

Quickly Benton connected up the cable to the one in the Land Rover. Yates meanwhile was on the R/T. 'Trap One to Greyhound over ...'

They heard the Brigadier's voice. 'Receiving you loud and clear, Trap One. Over.'

Yates glanced at Benton who nodded. 'All fixed up, sir.'

Yates spoke into the R/T. 'Eyes down, look in!'

The Brigadier's voice crackled back. 'Never mind the comedy, Captain Yates. Are you ready or aren't you?'

'Sorry, sir. You should be getting a picture now ...'

The Brigadier was watching a small monitor screen in the main control room. On it appeared a clear picture of Axos—doing, as Benton had just observed, precisely nothing. 'Affirmative, Trap One. Maintain surveillance.'

The Brigadier put down the R/T set as Chinn bustled into the control room, a chicken sandwich still clutched in his hand. 'Brigadier, I demand full access to the communications equipment. Unless I'm allowed to send reports to the Minister, to the country, Britain will get the blame for all this.'

'You mean *you'll* get the blame,' said the Brigadier unpleasantly. 'And quite right too, Mr Chinn.'

'If you don't allow me access to the Ministry ...'

The Brigadier lost patience. 'We are in the middle of a major crisis, Mr Chinn, and I have more to worry about than your desire to whitewash yourself. Now, stay out of my way or I'll have you put under arrest.'

Chinn lapsed into an offended silence, wandering over to the picture window. In the laboratory below, the Doctor and the Master were busy dismantling the Particle Accelerator. Perched on laboratory stools, Jo and Filer were chatting quietly.

Jo couldn't help smiling at Filer's gloomy face. 'Cheer up, Bill! You look like a disappointed bloodhound.'

'All bloodhounds look disappointed. It's an occupational disease.'

'Why so gloomy? You've got your man!'

'Have I? I don't like it, Jo.'

'Nor do I. But all we can do is wait.'

Filer shook his head. 'I don't mean the hanging around—I'm used to that. Or even the Axos business. That seems to be out of our hands ...'

'Then what *is* worrying you?'

'*They* are.' He nodded across the laboratory. 'Look at 'em! Thick as thieves.'

The Master and the Doctor stood by the Particle Accelerator, talking in low voices as they worked. Filer muttered, 'I've got a feeling there's something going on. Something we're not supposed to know about.'

Jo said, loyally. 'Don't be silly, Bill. The Doctor's using the Master because he needs his help, that's all.'

Inwardly she wasn't so positive. She remembered her own early suspicions when the Doctor had taken such a sudden interest in Winser's work. And why *had* the Doctor wanted the TARDIS brought down to Nuton? She knew how bitterly he resented his exile to Earth. Any chance of escape would present a tremendous temptation. Was the Doctor ready to buy his freedom at *any* price? Even if it meant making a deal with the Master? The dismantling process completed, the Doctor and the Master carried a pile of electronic parts into the TARDIS, closing the door behind them. Filer looked at Jo. Her face was as worried as his own.

The Doctor unloaded his collection of electronic oddments onto the console and started sorting through them. The Master watched sardonically. 'I'm still waiting to hear this brilliant scheme of yours, Doctor.'

The Doctor looked mildly surprised. 'Don't tell me you fell for that too? There isn't one. There's no way of stopping Axos now. Things have gone too far.'

'Indeed? Then may I ask what we're doing here?'

'Isn't it obvious? If you can help me to get my TARDIS going, we can both escape.'

'Doctor! Are you actually suggesting an alliance?'

The Doctor whirled round. 'Why not?' he demanded with sudden passion. 'Do you really think I intend to end my days as a heap of dust—on the second rate planet of a third rate star?'

'What? You mean you're prepared to leave your precious Earth to the tender mercies of Axos?'

'Certainly. You know *why* I'm on Earth. My fellow Time Lords exiled me here.'

The Master stroked his beard thoughtfully. 'I see. But why should *I* help you?'

'Well—we *are* both Time Lords.'

'And mortal enemies, as you very well know! I'll need a better reason than that, Doctor.'

'Very well.' The Doctor's voice hardened. 'If you don't help me, I'll hand you back to UNIT. You'll be a prisoner on a doomed planet.'

'And you'll be doomed with me!'

The Doctor nodded. 'I'm very well aware of it. We escape together—or we die together!'

The Master was still unconvinced. 'Why so generous, Doctor? Why not hand me over to UNIT and escape yourself?'

The Doctor looked shamefaced. 'I can't. The Time Lords have put a block on my knowledge of Dematerialisation Theory.'

'Ah, I see. How very unfortunate.'

'Well,' said the Doctor. 'Make up your mind. Time's running out you know—for both of us. Death —or freedom? Which is it to be?'

11

The Feast of Axos

The Master looked thoughtfully at the Doctor. Was he really capable of such ruthless realism? But the logic of the Doctor's arguments was unanswerable. It pleased the Master to think that even the Doctor was ultimately selfish. 'Very well, Doctor. I accept.'

'Good. Well now, you're the mechanic. How *do* we get the TARDIS going again? What's the answer?'

The Master held up a complicated section of machinery. 'The answer, Doctor, is here—the trigger mechanism from the Particle Accelerator. It has the potential to supply the deficient elements of your dematerialisation circuit. With a little ingenuity I may be able to combine one with the other to produce a functioning whole. But it will take time.'

'Not too much time, I hope,' snapped the Doctor. 'Right, you get on with the repairs. I'll look after the Space/Time Co-ordinates. I've already fed the equations into the computer.'

'Once you'd have worked them out in your head, Doctor,' mocked the Master.

'Once I didn't need your help for anything,' said the Doctor bitterly. 'But times change.' He started to leave the TARDIS, returned and removed a component from the console. 'In case you finish *before* I get back. You might be tempted to leave without me!'

The Doctor left the TARDIS, slamming the door behind him. The Master chuckled, and started work.

Inside Axos, all was calmness and order once more. The attempt to conquer Time travel had been abandoned. Axos was going about its normal business —the total absorption of all life and energy from a living planet. The Voice whispered, 'Data indicates distribution now complete. Activate Nutrition Cycle.'

All over the world, scientists watched in horror as the Axonite they were studying began to *grow* ... soon it was smashing its way out of their laboratories and destroying all in its path. Now people remembered the warnings sent out by UNIT. But it was too late. The Axonite was on the move ...

'It's *surfacing*, sir. The whole thing's just ... coming up out of the ground!'

As Yates's voice crackled over the R/T Chinn, the Doctor and the Brigadier watched the scene on the monitor in fascinated horror. Like a gigantic jelly-fish, the heaving, quivering bulk of Axos was rising out of the ground. The mound had become an enormous hill, and it was still growing. Soon it would be as big as a mountain, big enough to engulf the whole Nuton Complex.

The Brigadier grabbed the R/T. 'Yates, Benton, pull out at once. Back to the Complex on the double.'

124

Yates's voice was more than a little shaky. 'With the greatest of pleasure, sir. Trap One out.'

The Brigadier put down the receiver. 'Well, Doctor, what happens now?'

The Doctor studied the swelling horror on the screen. 'Axos will begin feeding. First on direct energy sources, like this Complex, then on anything in its path. It will grow even more, and become more mobile. It will probably send out smaller units to protect itself ...'

The R/T crackled into life again. The Brigadier picked it up, and listened to the frantic voice on the other end. Then he said curtly, 'We're doing all we can. I'll keep you informed.' He flicked a switch and the set went silent. 'That was UNIT H.Q., Doctor. This stuff's on the rampage all over the world.'

Chinn was shaking with fright. 'Where will it end, Doctor? When will that *thing* leave us alone?'

'When there's nothing left for it to feed on, Mr Chinn. By that time unfortunately the surface of the Earth will be like the surface of the moon—dead!'

Sergeant Benton and Captain Yates sprinted for their Land Rover, trying not to look at the ever-growing bulk of Axos dominating the skyline behind them. Yates jumped into the driving seat, Benton climbed into the back. 'What about the equipment, sir?'

'Just cast off the cables. We'll have to abandon it all.' Benton obeyed, and Yates started the engine. 'Hold tight,' he yelled and jolted through the trees at top speed. They swerved out onto the road that led back to the Nuton Complex.

A line of waving-tentacled Axon monsters barred their path. Benton grabbed a Sten and sprayed bullets into the heaving mass. Yates slammed his foot down hard and the Land Rover ploughed straight through the Axons, sending them flying in all directions.

The Land Rover sped on. Benton yelled, 'Think we've lost 'em, sir?'

Yates shook his head. 'They'll probably try again. Get those grenades ready just in case.'

There was a crackle of energy from the woods beside the road and an enormous tree toppled straight across their path. The Land Rover screeched to a halt. Benton looked behind them. The pursuing Axons were coming up fast. He lobbed a grenade, and blew the nearest into twitching fragments. But more Axons were emerging from the woods ...

Yates swung the Land Rover in a tight curve and drove back the way they'd come, while Benton flung grenades to clear their path. Some of the trees were on fire now, and smoke drifted across the road. A circle of Axons was closing in on the car.

Yates put his foot down again and drove straight into the ring of Axons, smashing a way through yet again.

As they sped down the road Benton yelled, 'I think we've made it, sir. We're through!' A tentacle groped down from above—one of the Axon monsters was sprawled on the canvas hood.

Yates shouted, 'Time to abandon ship! Jump!' Deliberately he swung the Land Rover into a ditch. Yates and Benton leaped from their seats just before the vehicle struck. They landed beside the road, rolling over and over to break their fall. They picked themselves up and looked back. The Land Rover had turned over and the Axon was trapped beneath it, tentacles thrashing frantically.

Benton ran forward a few paces and lobbed his last grenade with deadly accuracy. The grenade rolled inside the wrecked Land Rover, exploding seconds later. There was a crump and the Land Rover went up in a roar of flame.

Yates drew a gasping breath. 'Don't know what the Brig'll say about that, Sergeant Benton!'

Benton grinned. 'Me neither, sir. But at least we got one of them! What do we do now, sir?'

'We try to make it back to the Brigadier—on foot!'

Jo came into the laboratory, a long strip of computer print-out in her hand. She was studying the figures in puzzlement when the Doctor emerged from the TARDIS and took them from her. 'Ah, thank you, Jo. Just what I was waiting for!'

'Those figures, Doctor ...'

'Yes, Jo?' The Doctor paused in the TARDIS doorway. Was she wrong or was there something furtive in his manner?

'What are they, exactly?'

'Oh, just a few course co-ordinates,' said the Doctor vaguely.

Filer came to join them. 'Why *course* co-ordinates? Not going anywhere—are you, Doc?'

The Master appeared in the doorway of the TARDIS. Quickly the Doctor passed him the figures, saying, 'Everything ready?'

'As a matter of fact, it is.' The Master looked curiously at the Doctor, wondering how he would react now that the moment of decision had finally come. The Doctor hesitated.

Deliberately the Master raised his voice. 'Time we were on our way, Doctor!' Just as he'd hoped, the words provoked a crisis. Filer snatched out his gun.

'Not if I can help it!' he yelled.

But the Master's laser gun was already in the Doctor's hand. Before Filer could level his gun, the Doctor had him covered. 'Drop it please, Mr Filer.' Filer obeyed and the Doctor kicked the gun out of reach.

Heart-brokenly Jo said, 'Oh, Doctor ...'

The Doctor looked away, as the Brigadier came clattering down the ladder. 'Doctor, we're being attacked! Main gate says the Axons are swarming everywhere ...'

'Ah, there you are, Brigadier. Just in time to say goodbye!'

'But, Doctor, you can't ...' cried Jo.

'I'm afraid we must, Jo.'

'We?'

The Doctor gestured towards the Master. 'After all, we are both Time Lords. Goodbye, Jo. Goodbye, Brigadier.' He stepped inside the TARDIS.

The Master was already busy at the console. 'Neatly done, Doctor. You know, I never really thought you'd go through with it.'

'If we're going, let's go,' snapped the Doctor. 'If we *can* go, that is.'

The Master smiled. His hands flew over the console. Slowly and uncertainly at first, the central column of the TARDIS began its rise and fall.

From outside the laboratory came the rattle of gunfire, and the thud of grenades. There were shouted orders, dying screams. The sounds became louder. The battle was moving closer ...

Jo pounded on the TARDIS door, tears streaming down her face. 'You can't go, Doctor. You can't ... We need you ...' The blue light on top of the police box began flashing steadily and a wheezing, groaning sound filled the air.

A weary figure staggered into the laboratory, uniform grimy, face black with smoke. It took Filer a moment or two to recognise Captain Yates. Yates saluted hurriedly. 'The whole Complex is being over-run, sir. Those Axon things chased us right back here.'

Sergeant Benton followed him into the lab. 'They're right on top of us, sir. I've gathered a few of the lads.'

The Brigadier took charge. 'All right, Benton, get them in here.'

'Right, sir.' Benton dashed out to reappear seconds later with a handful of UNIT troops.

The Brigadier barked, 'Close the doors and get those blast-doors across.' Besides the everyday doors, the laboratory had additional blast-doors of heavy reinforced concrete. They were kept folded back, used only during particularly dangerous experiments. The UNIT soldiers worked hard heaving them into place.

Suddenly Yates noticed the groaning, light-flashing TARDIS.

'What's happening, sir? Where's the Doctor off to?'

'You can forget about the Doctor,' said the Brigadier curtly. 'He's no longer involved in our problems. Get the men into cover, and watch those doors!'

The TARDIS's groaning rose to a higher pitch, the light flashed brighter. Jo found herself pounding on thin air. The TARDIS had vanished. Filer led the sobbing Jo to cover.

They heard a rattle of gunfire from outside the laboratory, and a chilling scream as some unlucky straggler was destroyed by the Axons.

There was a terrifying silence. With no real hope, but with a determination not to give in, the Brigadier and the rest of the besieged waited for the final battle.

The Doctor thrust the Master away from the TARDIS console and began operating the controls. The Master tried to drag him off, but suddenly the little laser gun was in the Doctor's hand. 'Just be sensible, old chap ... I didn't tell you *all* my plan, you know.'

The Master saw the central column begin to slow down. 'You can't dematerialise here,' he screamed. 'We've scarcely moved—we're not even in Space/ Time!'

'Nevertheless, this is as far as we're going—for the moment.'

'But where are we?'

The Doctor grinned. 'Don't worry. You'll recognise it when you see it.' The central column stopped. 'Here we are then. Come on!'

Reluctantly the Master stepped outside. The first

thing that met his eye was his own TARDIS. He turned to find himself gazing into the single Eye. They were in the Brain area—back inside Axos.

The Master heard the familiar whispering voice. 'Why have you returned, Time Lords?' Tentacled Axon monsters appeared to surround them.

The Master shrugged. 'You'd better ask my friend here.'

'It's really very simple,' announced the Doctor. 'I've realised how invincible is the power of Axos. I'm prepared to give you the power of Time travel on one condition.'

'Well?'

'That you take Axos to Gallifrey, the planet of the Time Lords. I mean to take my revenge on those who exiled me—by destroying their planet.'

'If we agree—how can you keep your promise?'

'All we have to do is link drive systems. The TARDIS will become part of Axos. Axos itself will become a TARDIS.'

The Master looked at the Doctor in horror. Clearly the fellow's exile had affected his brain. An attack on the Time Lords themselves was beyond even the Master's audacity. How the Doctor must hate those who had captured and exiled him!

The Master panicked. 'This has nothing to do with me,' he shouted. 'My part is finished. All I ask is the return of my TARDIS. I leave you to your new alliance, Doctor.'

As he headed for the gleaming white dome the Doctor shouted, 'Stop him. I need his help for the setting-up of the link.'

A line of Axons barred the Master's way 'Help

him,' ordered the Voice of Axos. 'You may have your freedom when the link is finished.' Slowly the Master followed the Doctor back inside the TARDIS.

Crouching in what little cover they could find, the Brigadier and his party stared at the concrete door. For some time now they had heard the crackle of energy as the Axons outside the laboratory sought a way in. Suddenly a tiny glowing spot appeared in the centre of the concrete door. It turned into a tiny hole. A hole which grew steadily larger. Somehow the Axons had focussed their energy into a kind of thermic lance ...

Yates said, 'They'll soon be through, sir.'

The Brigadier's voice was calm. 'All right, everyone. Be ready with the grenades.'

When the hole was about a foot in diameter, it stopped growing.

Jo whispered to Filer. 'What's happening, Bill? Why have they stopped?'

Chinn mopped his streaming brow. 'Surely we ought to try and negotiate a surrender?' No one listened to him.

An arc of blazing light shot from the hole in the door to the Particle Accelerator. Immediately the half-wrecked machine started humming with power.

The Brigadier moved across to Ericson. 'What's happening?'

'They've managed to energise the Particle Accelerator. Look at the readings!' There was terror in Ericson's voice.

The Brigadier studied the dials on the control console—every dial was creeping up to maximum. 'Can't you shut it off?' he shouted.

'Not without the trigger mechanism. Your friend the Doctor took that!'

'So what'll happen?' The hum of power was rising to a roar.

'The particles will just go on accelerating and accelerating until—bang! The whole place will go up!'

Yates tugged at the Brigadier's arm, raising his voice above the throb of power. 'Look, sir. The door.'

The hole had begun growing again. Many-tentacled figures could be seen massing on the other side.

The roar of the runaway Particle Accelerator rose higher still . . .

12

Trapped in Time

The Master straightened up. 'There—it's finished! Your link's complete.'

'Not quite!' Thrusting the Master aside, the Doctor began adjusting controls at feverish speed, his hands flickering over the console like some demented pianist.

The Master watched him, a light of dawning comprehension in his eyes. 'Why are you changing the settings? That's a Time loop! Doctor, don't switch on—we'll be trapped too ...'

The Master tried to pull the Doctor away, but a hearty shove sent him reeling out through the still-open door of the TARDIS. Quickly the Doctor closed the doors. He touched the controls and the materialisation noise began.

Outside in the Brain area the Master yelled, 'Stop him, you fools! Don't you understand? He's committing suicide and taking us with him. It's all a trick. He's doing this for Earth, not you ... He's putting you in a Time loop and you'll stay there—forever!'

Even if the Axons had been prepared to listen to him, they were in no state to act. The sudden wrench through Time had totally disorientated them. They staggered wildly about the Brain area, tentacles flail-☞ helplessly. The Eye revolved furiously on its stalk. 'Stop them! Stop them!' screamed the Voice of Axos.

The Master thrust his way through the Axons and disappeared inside his TARDIS.

The Doctor leaned over the TARDIS console like a man setting a reluctant horse to a jump. 'Come on, old girl,' he muttered. 'You can do it. Don't let me down now. We've got to drag Axos into that Time loop!'

He flicked more switches and a final surge of power poured through the TARDIS ...

The concrete door crumbled away, and a flood of Axon monsters poured into the laboratory. The UNIT troops hurled their last grenades. The wave of Axons checked, they surged forward again.

Jo screamed as an Axon loomed over her. The Brigadier emptied his revolver into another, and he flung the gun in a last, useless gesture.

Yates and Benton lashed out, using empty rifles like clubs. Filer grabbed a lab stool and raised it above his head.

The Axons vanished.

Axos vanished. The heaving mountainous mass disappeared into thin air.

All over the world, the rampaging masses of Axonite vanished too.

In the Space/Time continuum Axos traced an un-ending spiral course, whirling forever in an endless figure-eight.

Inside his TARDIS the Doctor readjusted controls once more. 'Come on, old girl. One final effort! We must break free. You got them *in* the Time loop— now get me *out!*'

From outside the TARDIS he could hear the Voice of Axos. 'Your sacrifice will not save you, Time Lord. You are joined to us forever in the loop of Time. Your fate is ours!'

'Come on,' urged the Doctor. *'Come on!'*

The Eye of Axos glared in hopeless malignant rage as the TARDIS dematerialised.

And Axos continued its journey through Space/ Time—a journey that would never end ...

It took the dazed survivors only a moment to realise that although the menace of the Axons was gone, the menace of the roaring Particle Accelerator was still on top of them.

'Outside, everybody,' yelled the Brigadier. 'It'll go up any minute!'

Chinn led the dash to the door by several yards. They made it just in time. Even as they all got through the door there came the first explosion. Its force caved in most of the outer wall, and the entrance behind them was blocked by falling rubble.

Ericson grabbed the Brigadier's arm. 'Come on,' he shouted. 'That was only the first one. There'll be a whole series of them before it finally blows!' They ran for shelter.

In the laboratory, there was a wheezing, groaning noise. Blue light flashing, the TARDIS materialised. The door opened and the Doctor stepped out beaming. 'Hullo, everybody, I'm ...' His smile faded as he took in the desolation around him, the shuddering, roaring Accelerator.

There was an explosion and then another. Part of the roof caved in and the TARDIS was showered with rubble. 'Dear me,' said the Doctor mildly, and ducked hurriedly back inside.

He ran to the console and quickly operated controls. For a moment nothing happened. The TARDIS rocked with the force of another, greater explosion. 'Come on,' begged the Doctor. 'Take me somewhere—anywhere!'

Slowly the central column began to move ...

As a final terrifying explosion destroyed the laboratory forever, the TARDIS dematerialised yet again ...

Ericson led them to the shelter of one of the specially constructed blast-walls which surrounded the laboratory area. Almost immediately they were thrown to the ground by the final, shattering explosion. Ears ringing they looked out from shelter. There was a smoking, rubble-filled crater where once the laboratory had stood. Slowly they walked towards it.

Jo's face was white. 'What about the Doctor? Suppose he decided to come back after all and materialised inside the lab?'

The Brigadier shook his head. 'Let's hope he didn't, Jo. Nothing could have survived that.'

As if to prove him wrong there came a familiar groaning sound. The TARDIS re-materialised, balanced precariously on top of the heap of rubble. The door opened and the Doctor stepped out. Perched on a shattered beam, he looked down at the astonished faces below him. 'Well, there's a fine welcome, I must say!'

Much, much later, back in Hardiman's office, the Doctor was still trying to explain. 'It's perfectly simple, Brigadier. A Time loop is, well—it's a Time loop.' He made a complicated figure-of-eight gesture with his hands. 'You pass continually through the same fixed points in Space/Time.'

'And that's what Axos is doing?'

'That's right. For ever and ever. They wanted Time travel—and now they've got it!'

There was just one question occupying Filer. 'What about the Master?'

'I sincerely hope he's trapped in Axos too.'

'Hope?'

The Doctor looked a little uneasy. 'I can't be absolutely sure,' he said defensively. 'I was a little busy at the time!'

Filer just looked at him.

The Doctor cleared his throat. 'I'm ninety per cent certain, though.'

'How much?'

'Well, pretty certain. Fairly positive, really.' Faced with Filer's unwinking stare the Doctor threw up his hands. 'Oh, I suppose it's possible he got away—just possible.'

Filer heaved a deep, deep sigh.

The Brigadier took up the questioning. 'So how did you get out of this—Time loop thingummy?'

'I boosted the temporal circuits and broke free,' said the Doctor impatiently. 'Nearly blew up the TARDIS—but the old girl made it in the end.'

Now it was Jo's turn. 'Never mind the scientific stuff, Doctor. Why did you have us all think you'd made a deal with the Master to do the dirty on us?'

The Doctor put an arm round her shoulders. 'I'm sorry about all that, Jo—really! But I needed the Master's help—and I knew he'd never give it unless he thought I was as big a villain as he was!'

'Why didn't you let us into the secret?'

'I didn't dare. It was just because all your reactions were genuine that the Master was finally convinced.'

Jo smiled with relief. 'So you wouldn't really have gone off and left us in the lurch?'

The Doctor looked rather uncomfortable. 'To be perfectly honest, Jo ... Yes and no!'

Jo was indignant. 'And what does that mean?'

'Well *yes*, I would have gone off—but *no*, I wouldn't have left you in the lurch. I had a sort of double plan, you see. First to dispose of Axos—which I did. Then to get away from Earth in the TARDIS.'

'Which you didn't,' said Jo. 'Why not? A change of heart?'

The Doctor looked even more guilty. 'I'm afraid not, Jo. The Time Lords have programmed a return circuit into the TARDIS. Even if I do get it going, it will just take me back to Earth. I seem to be some kind of cosmic yo-yo,' he concluded indignantly.

Filer stood up. 'Well, goodbye, everyone. The disappointed bloodhound will now trail back to Washington.' He shook his head ruefully. 'And to think I reckoned England would be dull.'

After a round of handshakes, and a kiss on the cheek from Jo, Filer went on his way.

The Brigadier stood up too. 'Well, we'd better be getting back to UNIT H.Q. Make sure Chinn doesn't grab all the credit.'

Chinn was already safely back in Whitehall, explaining to the Minister how *his* genius had solved the problem.

The Doctor was looking out of the window, watching Yates, Benton and a squad of UNIT troops trying to get the TARDIS off its pile of rubble and onto a waiting lorry. They were using a rickety-looking improvised derrick, made from ropes and wooden beams. The TARDIS gave a sudden lurch, and the Doctor uttered an indignant yell. 'Hey, just you be careful with that—it's the only one I've got!'

Cloak flying behind him, he dashed out of the room, obviously determined to supervise operations himself.

The Brigadier collected his hat, gloves and swagger-stick. 'Come along, Miss Grant. It looks as if we'll have the Doctor with us for some time yet. Good job we've got you to keep an eye on him!'

Jo smiled to herself. Maybe the Doctor would defeat the Time Lords and get away from Earth—some day. She couldn't help hoping that it wouldn't happen too soon.

She crossed to the window. The Doctor had joined the little group around the pile of rubble, together with Sergeant Benton and Captain Yates. All three were arguing furiously, waving their arms, disputing the next move in rescuing the TARDIS. The Brigadier joined them, and the arguments broke out afresh. Jo grinned, and went down the stairs to join in. It was nice to see things back to normal . . .

DOCTOR WHO

	DAVID WHITAKER	
0426101103	Doctor Who and The Daleks	£1.50
042611244X	TERRANCE DICKS Doctor Who and The Dalek Invasion of Earth	£1.25
0426103807	Doctor Who and The Day of the Daleks	£1.35
042620042X	Doctor Who – Death to the Daleks	£1.35
0426119657	Doctor Who and The Deadly Assassin	£1.25
0426200969	Doctor Who and The Destiny of the Daleks	£1.35
0426108744	MALCOLM HULKE Doctor Who and The Dinosaur Invasion	£1.35
0426103726	Doctor Who and The Doomsday Weapon	£1.35
0426201464	IAN MARTER Doctor Who and The Enemy of the World	£1.25
0426200063	TERRANCE DICKS Doctor Who and The Face of Evil	£1.25
0426201507	ANDREW SMITH Doctor Who – Full Circle	£1.35
0426112601	TERRANCE DICKS Doctor Who and The Genesis of the Daleks	£1.35
0426112792	Doctor Who and The Giant Robot	£1.25
0426115430	MALCOLM HULKE Doctor Who and The Green Death	£1.35

Prices are subject to alteration

DOCTOR WHO

0426116909	Doctor Who and The **Mutants**	£1.25
0426201302	Doctor Who and The **Nightmare of Eden**	£1.25
0426112520	Doctor Who and The **Planet of the Daleks**	£1.25
0426116828	Doctor Who and The **Planet of Evil**	£1.25
0426106555	Doctor Who and The **Planet of the Spiders**	£1.25
0426201019	Doctor Who and **The Power of Kroll**	£1.35
0426116666	Doctor Who and The **Pyramids of Mars**	£1.25
042610997X	Doctor Who and The **Revenge of the Cybermen**	£1.25
0426200926	IAN MARTER Doctor Who and **The Ribos Operation**	£1.35
0426200616	TERRANCE DICKS Doctor Who and The **Robots of Death**	£1.25
042611308X	MALCOLM HULKE Doctor Who and The **Sea Devils**	£1.35
0426116586	PHILIP HINCHCLIFFE Doctor Who and The **Seeds of Doom**	£1.25
0426200497	IAN MARTER Doctor Who and The Sontaran **Experiment**	£1.25
0426110331	MALCOLM HULKE **Doctor Who and The Space War**	£1.35
0426201337	TERRANCE DICKS Doctor Who and The **State of Decay**	£1.35

Prices are subject to alteration

STAR Books are obtainable from many booksellers and newsagents. If you have any difficulty please send purchase price plus postage on the scale below to:-

Star Cash Sales
P.O. Box 11
Falmouth
Cornwall
OR
Star Book Service,
G.P.O. Box 29,
Douglas,
Isle of Man,
British Isles.

While every effort is made to keep prices low, it is sometimes necessary to increase prices at short notice. Star Books reserve the right to show new retail prices on covers which may differ from those advertised in the text or elsewhere.

Postage and Packing Rate
UK: 45p for the first book, 20p for the second book and 14p for each additional book ordered to a maximum charge of £1.63. BFPO and EIRE: 45p for the first book, 20p for the second book, 14p per copy for the next 7 books thereafter 8p per book. Overseas: 75p for the first book and 21p per copy for each additional book.